It's Sauce, Not Gravy!

The Ingredient That Changes Everything for Gio

J. A. Marz

Printed in the United States of America
Publisher: JAM 3 Strategic Marketing & PR, LLC
Published in Easton, PA
Cover design by 100 Covers
Edited by Christine A. Krahling, The Reading Life
Interior design by Sara DeGonia | DeGoniaEditing.com

ISBN-13: 979-8-9867483-1-3 (ebook)
ISBN-13: 979-8-2189117-6-8 (paperback)

*To all those on the journey to self-discovery:
The road is paved like the Roman Appian
Way—bumpy. Embrace the ride, nurture it,
and smooth it out for others.*

Chapter 1

What a Beautiful Thing, a Sunny Day

Daydreaming was a favorite pastime for Gio Marzo, the writer. He would routinely escape in thought, and the quiet time sparked ideas while the words magically scrolled on a ticker across his brain. "Get it down, get it on the record before you lose it, dumbass," he would scold himself.

It was that sort of day, the beginning, with him in a deep trance in his writing studio above the courtyard of La Terre Felice. He was now the patriarch of the Tuscan agriturismo, supported by his two modern-day mamma nonnas, Gabby's mother Antoinette Rosetti, and his mother, Isabella Maranzzano.

A young Gio always knew where to find a meal. Back then, his grandmother, Nonna Madeline, cooked on most days, a slave to the traditions and expectations of hard-core Italian bloodlines.

Gio's grandfather, Giovanni, was no exception. European immigrants brought their culture and traditions with them from their homeland when they arrived in the U.S. in the early twentieth century. They didn't just bring it—they bred it, one stubborn generation at a time. It was a hard life, but it was simple.

After a full day of backbreaking labor cutting stone, Giovanni's physical exertion worked up a healthy appetite for the freshest ingredients he could grow in the garden. The laborer also produced a strong vintage…a homemade red in his wine cellar every year.

While the culture was the siren call, the taste of life was undeniably spectacular.

"Hey, Prrrrince of Wales, Prrrrince of Wales," Giovanni would roar in broken English as young Gio made his entrance through the door. An obvious reference, of course, to Prince Charles at the time in England. This became the announced anthem whenever Madeline and Giovanni's pride and joy arrived in a room.

"Mad-e-lin, your grandson needs to eat," Giovanni would say, while enjoying a healthy swig of vino rosso and showing a brown-toothed grin from ear to ear. *"Mangia, mangia, Gianni!"*

"Nonna…some sauce and bread," commanded Gio. "Are the meatballs ready yet?"

Oh, they tried to teach me to speak Italian, he thought to himself, but he wanted no part of the language of amore. Right then, it was a language of love for food.

The heady aroma of crushed garlic, olive oil, freshly grated Pecorino Romano, and simmering veal and beef in the sauce would fill the air. Gio couldn't care or appreciate the time it took for Madeline's preparation, or why his mouth salivated in advance of the next best meal of his young life.

This was standard protocol any day of the week, especially Sunday, when the entire extended family gathered for one of Madeline's legendary feasts. Mixed greens with escarole drowned in an oil/vinegar concoction, stuffed artichokes, and, of course, plenty of pasta with braciole, meatballs, and Italian sausage, bought fresh the day before. After dinner, perhaps an anisette or limoncello to go with cake and roasted chestnuts.

The pasta dish would be different every time, but the flavor was eternal. The wine, of course, was strong. And, for special holidays like Easter or Gio's birthday, Madeline also made her grandson his special pan of 'man ni got' (manicotti).

Years later, Gio would remember those times as some of the best of his life, but not then. He was too antsy to appreciate anything.

Madeline was a Russo before being a Maranzzano, and Signore Giovanni knew when Madeline's brother Michael would be in town. She would cook and prepare to the point of exhaustion in advance of his arrival.

Young Gio liked Uncle Mike, who owned a villa in the Northeast U.S. that included a private Italian grotto with statue fountains and cherubs spitting water. The family gatherings at the Russo grotto were legendary. Giovanni senior usually ended the celebration by standing on the ornate steps and treating guests with a wine-induced, Caruso-like rendition of the Neapolitan anthem to a sunny day, "O Sole Mio."

"Che bella cosa na jurnata 'e sole,
n'aria serena doppo na tempesta!
Pe' ll'aria fresca pare gia' na festa
Che bella cosa na jurnata 'e sole.

Ma n'atu sole
cchiu' bello, oi ne'.
'O sole mio
sta 'nfronte a te!

*'O sole, 'o sole mio
sta 'nfronte a te,
sta 'nfronte a te!"*[*]

Madeline would get so embarrassed after a few choruses that she would send young Gio to fetch his grandfather and find him a seat to calm down, of course, with another glass of vino.

Happy, special times, but with all the lavish family affairs, there was a dark side. Uncle Mike's business enterprise was a bit shady, all exposed later in life after he lost everything in a high-stakes gambling scheme that backfired. His shenanigans were the reason Aunt Mary wore black the rest of her life.

Gio would routinely ask, "Nonna, why don't we go to Uncle Mike's anymore?" while drowning his freshly baked Tuscan bread in sauce. Madeline always answered the same. "Uncle Mike has been sick and not well."

Gio never understood the situation until many years later, after the old guard had all passed. While watching *The Godfather* for the first time for one of his writing assignments in a remote corner of Europe, he saw Uncle Mike.

---

[*]*"O Sole Mio,"* written in 1898 by Giovanni Capurro and Eduardo di Capua.

"Holy shit," he yelled aloud at the time. "Brando is Uncle Mike! My Uncle Mike lives as Vito Corleone!"

It was hilarious to everyone within earshot. Brando's appearance in the movie mirrored what Gio remembered about Uncle Mike…thin moustache, sagging jowls stuffed with something, and a raspy, deep commanding voice. When Uncle Mike spoke, everyone listened, especially Madeline…

Gio was ripped from his thoughts at that moment. Antoinette and Isabella were calling, but their tone was different…not panic, but urgent.

"Gio, Gio…" Antoinette yelled, standing at the courtyard door with something held close to her chest. "You need to see this. Now."

Gio rode down the steps from his studio and stepped outside. *"Cos'e`?"*

Antoinette held out an envelope. The handwriting stopped him cold. It was hers…Gabby's!

"This came in the mail today," Isabella whispered. "It's dated eleven months ago. She arranged to have it sent one year after…"

Gio took the envelope with shaking hands. Gabriella Rosetti was scrawled across the top corner, along with a Pienza postal stamp. Inside was a single sheet of her soft-pressed stationery and the faintest trace of her lavender perfume. Gio nearly fell to the floor.

"*Ciao amore mio,*" the letter began.

"*If you're reading this, it means I've been gone long enough for the vines to miss me, and for you to question everything. Good. That means you're still listening to your heart. But now it's time for something new. I've left you one more piece of myself…*"

The words blurred, and Gio blinked hard.

"She left a contact," Antoinette said softly. "A woman from Siena."

Gio looked back down at the letter. He didn't realize it, but he was holding his breath.

"*Promise me you'll let her in,*" the letter continued. "*She doesn't know everything yet, but she will. She's part of the story now.*"

So much for a sunny day, Gio thought.

Chapter 2

Oh Antoinette, I'm Looking for Your Secret Ingredient

It had been one year since Gabby's death. Gio, over that time, had thrown himself into keeping her memory alive as the heartbeat and soul of La Terre Felice. It was not easy, as Gabby had made her mark on everything she had ever touched, especially the Tuscan hills of the estate.

Gabby was an artist in every way…she choreographed life, fed the land and the people who worked with her and for her; the guests, and the local villagers who had been touched by her generosity and kindness. It was a canvas of life, of family, of history, of community, and now she was throwing some colors onto the palette that didn't quite seem to fit.

The letter stunned nearly everyone. Gio again lost himself in deep thought and mumbled to himself, "*Gabby, you trusted me with this place; I can't just open it up to some stranger."*

Antoinette looked as if she saw a ghost. Isabella watched quietly, her gaze on Gio. Gio still felt guilty over Gabby's illness, and he couldn't believe this was happening, but he owed it to Antoinette and the staff of La Terre Felice to do everything in his power to keep the vibrant agriturismo moving and active to honor Gabby.

Gabby's letter ended with, *"I know this is a shock to you, Gio, but be patient. When the time is right, contact Renata Buca at the small artisan shop next to Piazza del Campo in Siena. She will be expecting you. All my love, forever and a day. Gabby."*

Gio quickly concluded that this was his penance for being a vagabond and nearly losing La Terre Felice for the Rosetti family in a golf hustle. But for now, he needed to put all that aside and focus on the primary duty. The heavy tourist season was beginning, and the agriturismo needed the attention of a fully engaged staff. Gio would think and speak more when the time was right.

Antoinette quickly left the conversation and returned to the kitchen to be with her chefs. Isabella remained still, but her steady eyes stayed on Gio.

Antoinette was silent. That was unlike her. Gio suspected there was something more to the story because of Antoinette's reaction to the letter. He would have to deal with her later.

"Gio, what does this letter mean?" Isabella finally broke the silence, "I don't know, Mamma. But I will need to track down the letter and investigate," he replied.

As a writer, Gio knew all the tricks of the trade in research and tracking details. He would pour his energy into finding out what Gabby's surprise was all about and connecting the dots for some answers. But that would have to wait for now. He needed time to let the shock wave settle.

Gio knew all too well how Gabby worked and that she would orchestrate events to make life interesting. Now, she was doing that from the afterlife at La Terre Felice. Gio chuckled to himself. She was a beautiful minx and a fucking master planner.

Chapter 3

Gio's Sauce Needs a Little Sugar

Writing life can be solitary. And strange at times…always doubting the words. Do they have merit? Are they good enough? Growing up in an Italian family, Gio also felt the pressure of his masculinity in many ways. Writers and artists were softer, not seen as tough enough to carry a family name. Gio's great-grandfather and grandfather, both named Giovanni, were like comic book heroes reeking of strength from every pore.

Gio's father, Salvatore, couldn't compete, couldn't win his father's praise, so he abandoned Isabella and his son early in life. From that point, Gio was surrounded by strong and elegant Italian women who were extremely influential.

Those *gumadi* or BFFs of Madeline seemed to always overpraise and encourage young Gio, sometimes to the point of giving him the *"malocchio,"* the Italian evil eye hex, that's said to be fueled by a look of jealousy. Superstition, perhaps, but Gio would violently vomit each time they visited, which forced Madeline to grab the oil and water to pray her evil spirit prayers. This just pissed off Isabella to no end.

While Gio's grandfather wanted to teach him the art of stone masonry, Gio opted to investigate world cultures, different people, and unique lifestyles. He loved sports, especially golf and baseball, and those occupied much of his outside interests.

Food was life. "Make sure you send your grandson home for lunch," chimed Madeline to her husband each time Gio helped his grandfather build a new concrete front porch for a neighborhood row home.

"He's always yelling, Nonna, at me and the workers who bring in the cement," said Gio, savoring his lunchtime away from Giovanni. "I don't want to work for him anymore."

Gio took advice from Isabella and Madeline. Born on an Easter Sunday, under the Aries fire sign, he was a pioneer, an explorer, and always looked to embrace the burning flame of individuality in all aspects of life, especially to realize that Easter has not landed on his birthday since. Creativity, with the ability to put words together to tell a story quickly, became Gio's gift. He wanted no part of the heavy labor his grandfather endured throughout his working life.

Maybe he wasn't as tough as Giovanni expected him to be in the Italian community. Many of his childhood friends floated through school as poor students, only to become thugs and two-bit gangsters. But Gio knew he wanted a different calling, so he weathered the backlash and stayed true to himself.

Gio also never understood why his life developed into a wandering storyteller. He just gravitated to the freedom of solitude, independence, and chasing skirts. Meeting and losing Gabby, as well as running the agriturismo over the past year, opened his eyes to much more.

One recent evening in his studio, he caught a TV interview on the BBC with actor and musician Billy Bob Thornton, who was describing a similar life experience to Dan Rather.

Thornton said he was ridiculed by his father early in life because he wasn't as big and tough as his father wanted him to be. So he naturally sought refuge with a strong mother and grandmother, who were softer, more inquisitive about life, and more creative in developing relationships.

Thornton, the actor, didn't hate his father and even appreciated the poor experience for helping him find his way through life. Even though Gio's father abandoned the family, he didn't hate Sal, and certainly not his grandfather. They were men having to figure out how to grow a family the best way they knew how at the time. Be strong and exhibit a "take no shit from anyone" attitude. And, in the case of Gio's father, Sal, if you couldn't handle it, get the fuck out.

Gabby became another strong female influence in Gio's life. From the moment the two met in Rosa's trattoria in San Gimignano, he was hooked. Gabby was drop-dead gorgeous with a killer body and an all-out artistic DNA. A burning desire relentlessly camped out in Gio's groin from that point on. Gabby understood Gio completely.

"*Tu sei quello che sei*. I know you better than you know yourself, Gio," she would always say. "That's why I put up with your wandering ways."

The letter sent by Gabby a year after her passing was a bombshell. Gio would now have to use his creative skills to manage not only himself, but the team at La Terre Felice, the expectations of Antoinette and Isabella, and most importantly, the guests descending on the agriturismo for the summer months.

…And soon, he thought, his investigation into Renata Buca and what she means to this evolving story.

Chapter 4

The Hot Seasoning Begins at La Terre Felice

Golden sunlight was an assumed condition in the Tuscan countryside. It cracked slowly as the Tuscan hills were shrouded in a blanket of morning mist that held over the valley. It was a common sight this time of year. It started in early summer and moved well into the fall. As the day wore on, the light that danced across the vines in each row painted the animated land by a wave of God's hand.

Gio stood on the stone terrace above the vineyard with an espresso in hand. He watched as Luca Rossi, the head groundskeeper at La Terre Felice for more than a decade, shouted at the vineyard hands like a general conducting morning drills.

Luca was strong and weathered, but had the perfect personality to work his knowledge, empathetic support for his teams, and laser-sharp guidance for the agriturismo to be the showcased jewel in this area of Italy.

Gulping down the last shot of espresso, Gio understood just how important it was to have the land healthy, thriving, and alive. That's exactly what Gabby would have wanted.

The smell of freshly baked bread from Antoinette's kitchen mingled with the richness of the soil to validate that La Terre Felice was stirring, rocking, and buzzing with activity at the start of a new season.

Tourists trickled in by their rented Sport Fiats or private van drivers, wide-eyed and breathless with wonder, ready to exchange the pressures of their worlds for the simple indulgence of olives, wine, and the kind of food that made them believe in wholesome family values again, if only for a week or two.

Inside the kitchen, Antoinette bustled about with the grace of a once-in-a-generation Nonna. "Today we are making cavatelli pasta," she instructed, "Something with more substance for the guests after a long day of travel."

Antoinette presided over all the pasta making with her staff, taste-tested sauces with a practiced sweep of her wooden spoon and charmed the guests who wandered in looking for her secret recipes. She was fiercely protective of them. "Not for sale at any price," she snapped.

Isabella, quieter and more reserved, worked alongside her and the kitchen staff, carefully arranging olive oil tastings and setting up the terrace for the welcome feast in the evening.

As the season filled with life, Gio's mind wasn't nearly as harmonious. The letter. Renata. It all felt like unfinished business. Dragging on him like a three-foot par putt to win a lot of money.

Just then, the familiar thunder of an old Fiat Spider purred up the gravel drive.

Franco.

The car door creaked open, and the champion golfer stepped out like an Adonis in aviator sunglasses, a wide grin, and his golf bag riding shotgun in the passenger seat.

"Gio Marzo! Still can't believe you traded in your global jaunts for… what? Grape duty?" Franco teased, walking up the drive as if he lived there. Of course he did.

Gio smirked and pulled Franco into a quick embrace. "Yeah, well, the grapes don't hustle me for money like you do, *mio amico*," he said. "What brings you here now? Not busy enough trying to win something on the DP Tour?"

Franco shrugged, "Tour break. I've had a good year so far," he said proudly. "Needed fresh pasta, fresh air, good wine, and maybe…a little trouble."

"Good. You're just in time. We've got plenty of everything."

Franco and Gio walked together past tourists clicking photos, children chasing chickens, and the vineyard crew sprucing up before the afternoon tastings.

Franco soaked it in. "Gabby's touch is everywhere, Gio."

Gio's throat tightened, but he nodded. "Yeah. Everywhere."

Franco slapped him on the back. "So tell me more about this letter. And this Renata."

Gio exhaled a long breath. "I haven't started to dig in. But I have a feeling it's about to get deeper."

La Terre Felice thrived on welcoming strangers as family, friendships like brotherhood, feeding guests like royalty, and holding tight with its secrets, for now.

Chapter 5

A Round and a Revelation

Tuscany offered more than vineyards and old traditions. In comparison, Los Angeles, California, had more golf courses than the entire country of Italy, yet tucked quietly on the edge of the local Tuscan village was a rustic nine-hole course. It was the kind of place where the grass wasn't perfectly manicured, and the sand traps seemed more like suggestions than hazards.

Perfect for Gio and Franco.

"Seriously? You brought your clubs?" Gio laughed as Franco tossed his bag onto the cart.

"Did you think I came all this way for the wine?" Franco grinned, teeing up his ball. "I came to remind you how bad you are at this game, and how much money I can take."

The first hole was friendly enough. A short par four that welcomed lazy swings and easy conversation.

"So," Franco said, mid-backswing, "this letter from Gabby…this Renata Buca…what's the angle?"

Gio sliced his drive slightly to the right. "I don't know yet. It makes me nervous. Antoinette acted strangely. Feels…innocent enough. But something's off."

Franco crushed his ball down the middle. "Knowing Gabby, there is something behind this."

"Likely," Gio replied as he proceeded to smack a crisp 7-iron from the rough onto the green. "Gabby wouldn't send me to her unless she had a reason."

They played on, trading shots and ribbing each other on every hole in between, but the conversation always drifted back to the question at hand.

Franco leaned on his putter as Gio lined up a birdie attempt on the 9th green. "You've got instincts, Gio. Use 'em. You've written about con artists, real estate scams, and land grabs. Your experience means something here."

Gio sank the birdie putt with a lazy flick of his wrist. "Yeah, but it also feels like Gabby wanted me to trust her. And that's the part that's messing with me."

Franco smirked. "Sounds like you need backup. Lucky for you, I'm on vacation."

"Since when is playing golf in Tuscany considered work?"

"Since you made it complicated."

They shared a laugh, but the weight of it lingered.

Franco pulled his long birdie putt to the left, then tapped his ball into the cup for par. "Listen, we'll dig. Quietly," he said. "See what sticks to this girl's story. And if there's heat coming, we'll deal with it."

Gio nodded, grateful. "Ok, paisan. You owe me five euros!"

Heading back to La Terre Felice, they laughed like hell. Once again, Gio hustled the golf pro.

That evening, Gio and Franco sat on the stone terrace of the main house at La Terre Felice, an open bottle of Chianti between them.

The vineyard stretched out below and into the horizon. Luca's recent work to repair irrigation on the south field was well done and critically important to the vines due to the dry conditions early in the season. Sunshine is necessary for growing grapes, yet just the right amount of water is also important for a good vintage.

Gio traced the rim of his glass, staring at the land as if Gabby might walk out from between the vines at any moment.

"She's still everywhere, you know," Gio said, his voice low.

Franco swirled his wine. "Yeah. I can feel her here."

Silence settled between them, comfortable and heavy all at once.

Franco broke it. "You thinking of packing up again? Once this is all settled?"

Gio shook his head slowly. "I don't know. Part of me still wants to run. The other part feels chained here."

"Maybe it's not chains, Gio. Maybe it's roots."

They drank quietly.

Franco finally added, "This Renata thing…You're not alone in this."

Gio glanced sideways. "Since when did you become the voice of reason?"

Franco grinned. "Since I realized you always need someone to keep your ass out of trouble."

They clinked glasses as the sun melted behind the hills.

La Terre Felice pulsed with life all around them. Staff laughing in the kitchen, tourists savoring the last bites of dinner, the land breathing, growing, and nurturing others in perfect harmony.

Gio leaned back in his chair, briefly allowing peace to settle in.

Tomorrow will come, and with it, more questions.

Chapter 6

A Simmering Walk in the Vineyard

La Terre Felice had quieted down for an early summer night. The tourists sipped at their glasses of wine, the kitchen had a clatter of Antoinette's crew cleaning up and putting away, and the soft buzz of nighttime took over the vineyard.

Isabella made her rounds alone. She didn't know what she was running after. Perhaps a little air.

She had come for Gio, of course. But in some way, the place had worked its way under her skin. She had never met Gabby, but Gabby's fingerprints were everywhere. People still said you could feel her in the cottage walls, in the soil, in the way the vines seemed to stand a little taller.

"Signora Isabella," Luca's voice drifted from the next row over.

She turned as he emerged from between the vines, shaking his hands on a rag.

"An evening *passeggiata?*" he inquired, falling into step beside her.

"Some places don't let you sleep. A stroll helps me relax."

Luca nodded slightly. "Gabby used to say the vines whispered their best secrets at night."

Isabella smirked. "I never met her, you know. I only know her through Gio, and what this place has meant to so many."

"That's the version that matters," Luca said. "La Terre Felice, this region, these people have a way of doing that to you. Dives into people's souls unannounced, gets between your toes and never leaves, whether you like it or not."

The two continued the stroll in comfortable silence, the type that didn't need to fill every space with words.

"I missed a lot of Gio's life," Isabella finally murmured. "Always thought I'd make it up to him out there somewhere. I had to come to Italy to see him."

Luca paused near an ancient olive tree, leaning back against a fence post. "Gabby would've liked you, Isabella," he told her. "You don't dress things up."

She shot him a look. Her voice even. "Maybe you can show me how this place breathes. How to take care of it the right way."

"I can do that," he said, plain as that.

No grand proclamations. No promises.

As they made their way back towards the main house, Isabella felt something shift. Not a fire of new love, but a quiet companionship she had not realized she was missing.

The land had a way of making things grow, after all.

Perhaps they too.

Chapter 7

A Secret Escapes

It was one of those rare, quiet early afternoons at La Terre Felice. The last of the guests had gone, and the new ones wouldn't arrive until morning.

Gio found Antoinette in the kitchen, her hands deep in dough, working in a slow, steady rhythm.

He waited a beat, then spoke softly.

"Antoinette, we need to talk. About the letter."

Her hands didn't stop. "So talk."

"You knew about this…about Renata," he said.

Antoinette's fingers pressed deeper into the dough. "There are some things we think we can leave in the past, Gio. Some things we bury for a reason."

"Gabby wanted me to find Renata. She left that for me."

Antoinette finally looked at him. Her eyes were calm, but there was something locked behind them.

"She left it for you because in the end, she trusted you, Gio," Antoinette said. "Even with all your travels and your absence, she always trusted you."

Gio softened. "Did you know about her? Renata? About why Gabby never said anything?"

Antoinette wiped her hands on a towel, stalling. "Gabby… had a life before all this. Before you. Before La Terre Felice was what it is now."

"A life in Florence?"

Antoinette's shoulders tensed, just a fraction. "She went there for school. She was young, a teenager. She was…"

She paused, shifting the bowl aside. "There was someone. A man. The wrong kind who took advantage of her."

Gio waited yet wanted to press hard. His insides raged, but he remained respectful.

Antoinette kept her gaze low. "Someone tied to business in the gold trade. She worked for him at the Ponte Vecchio. You don't need to know his name."

"I do," Gio said quietly. "Antoinette, you know I do research and investigate for my writing. Eventually, I will find out his name."

Antoinette shook her head, her eyes welled up, and she was about to lose it emotionally. "Some names aren't worth remembering, Gio."

He let that hang there.

"Gabby left that life behind," she added. "She came home after her schooling and work at the University. She supported Antonio and me. She then helped us build this place. Over the years, she resisted other men, and you, Gio, at first. Then built you and brought you back."

Gio nodded. "Why didn't she tell me?"

"She didn't want the weight of that old story to follow her here. She didn't want it to follow you."

She ran out of time, he thought to himself.

Antoinette gave a soft, knowing smile. "Gabby always found a way to finish what she started. Even now."

Gio stayed in the kitchen, eyes on the floor, his mind chewing on the information overload.

There was still more Antoinette wasn't saying. He could feel it.

But he wasn't going to force it. Not yet.

This sauce needed more time to simmer.

Chapter 8

Processing Secret Ingredients

Later that afternoon, the terrace outside the main house was quiet, but the hum of work carried across La Terre Felice as usual.

Maria, the estate's head housekeeper, was preparing fresh linens for the guest cottages. Paolo was repairing a damaged stone wall along the driveway entrance that one of the guest vehicles had accidentally backed into. Sofia's laugh drifted from her office window while meeting with an agency creative team planning the new marketing campaign. Sofia wasn't sure Gio would approve, but what the hell, she knew how to push him to the edge of agreement.

The La Terre Felice machine kept moving forward, even when Gio's head was elsewhere.

Franco, after a mid-afternoon workout, found Gio sitting at the table, two glasses already poured.

"You didn't have to wait for me," Franco said, sliding into the chair across from him.

Gio was in awe of how smooth Franco moved. Graceful, unpretentious, dripping with charisma. Yet for all that likeable softness, he was a killer inside. That's what made him a great golfer. He knew how to finish.

"Figured you'd show up," Gio said. "You always do."

Franco took a sip. "So, are you going to tell me what Antoinette said, or do I have to guess?"

Gio stared at his glass of wine. "She told me just enough to screw with my head. Gabby's past. Florence. Some man tied to the gold trade at the Ponte Vecchio."

Franco raised an eyebrow. "Gold trade? That's not a side hustle. That's big time, Gio."

"She didn't give me a name. Just said Gabby left that life behind. That's all I got."

Franco set his glass down. "You know that's not all there is."

"Fucking right," Gio shot back.

"You thinking what I'm thinking?"

"That this isn't just about some old flame? Yeah."

Franco smirked. "With you, it never is. This sauce is starting to burn."

Gio shook his head, almost smiling. "I believe there's a daughter, Franco. Gabby's daughter. Antoinette didn't spell it out, but it's there between the lines. She was so young, and someone, this unknown guy, took advantage of her."

Franco leaned forward. "So why now? Why send you that letter?"

"She wanted me to connect with Renata. I don't know why—yet."

Franco leaned back, stretching. "Maybe she needs something. Maybe you do."

Gio didn't answer right away.

Franco held back at first, then nudged him. "So what's next?"

"Siena."

Franco grinned. "Finally. A real city."

"You just want a golf day and probably get some early insight into a bet for the Palio."

The Palio di Siena was a thrilling, historic bareback horse race held twice a year in Siena's main square, Piazza del Campo—known simply as Il Campo to the locals. Most of the city's seventeen districts (called Contrade) compete in a fierce race around the square for bragging rights in less than 90 seconds. It's part of the history and tradition of Sienese culture. The Palio doesn't have an official betting system, yet the

Contrade conduct unofficial bets to bribe and manipulate the race's outcome. The jockeys are hired guns, too, so they can be bought and influenced by competing districts. All so typical Italian.

"Gotta keep the swing sharp during my break. Besides, you need me for this."

Gio clinked his glass against Franco's. "Yeah. I do, paisan."

As they sat in comfortable silence, Maria passed by with folded towels, and Paolo finished his work before heading to the barn across the courtyard. Sofia shouted something from the office about making sure Gio finished his prep for an upcoming travel podcast.

The place was alive. Moving. Waiting for its next story.

And so were they.

Chapter 9

The Primi Piatti—a First Course

The drive to Siena was silent, but Franco was in no mood to let the quiet last for any great length.

"You're a lot calmer for a guy who's about to knock on the door of possibly Gabby's daughter," Franco said as he dug in his clutch to make the turn, his shades already in place.

"I'm not calling her that," Gio said, never looking away from the road. "Not yet. Maybe not ever."

"Sure you aren't," Franco said with a grin. "Just a little recon mission. Nothing personal."

The car pulled up on the edge of Il Campo. Gio had always loved Siena – the grit, the tight turns, the lean of the buildings and their fashionista chain shops as they embraced each district and seemed to watch over the tourists who trudged by on their way to the square.

Franco found a golf shop carved into one of the side streets and grinned. "After we locate her, I am picking up some new gloves. Priorities, my friend."

Gio rolled his eyes but said nothing.

The artisan shop Gabby had written about was in one of the side alleys off the Piazza, that sort of forgotten place that you could walk right by. Gio pushed the door open, and the smell of leather and dust hit him as he entered.

The young woman behind the counter looked up but did not even bother with a smile. She didn't have to. Gio got it right away.

"Renata Buca?" Gio said, his voice steady.

"That's me." She kept on working, setting up a display of small leather journals.

"I'm Gio Marzo. This is Franco Reno."

She offered a nod but nothing more. "You here to buy something or just going through your repertoire of Italian names?"

Franco laughed. Gio did not.

"I'm here because… someone asked me to find you." Her eyes flicked up, and that's when it caught him. The eyes. Gabby's eyes. That piercing blue that could melt an iceberg. It hit him hard. Same dark hair, same sharp beauty that didn't try to be beautiful. She couldn't stage it any better. The resemblance was breathtaking, like a gut punch. He didn't let it show.

"Yeah? Who?" she said, entirely unmoved.

"Gabriella Rosetti."

Her hands stopped for half a beat, then returned to motion. "I've heard the name."

"She left me a letter. Told me to come here. To find you."

Renata raised an eyebrow, no fan of this encounter so far, and still sizing up these strangers. "Okay. You found me. Now what?"

Gio was not used to being stonewalled. "I was hoping you could tell me."

"I don't have much to say about Gabriella Rosetti. She was part of a story I don't tell."

Franco leaned against a shelf with his arms crossed, taking it all in.

"Look," Gio said, "I'm not here to throw up on your life. I'm not here to drag anything up you don't want me to. You can trust that."

"You're doing a pretty good job of it anyway, *stronzo*."

Fair enough. Gio thought that. And not the sort of attitude he was unused to, either.

"She told me to find you. That's all I know. She told me you would be waiting."

Renata shrugged half-heartedly. "Funny. I wasn't waiting for anyone."

"She said you would be."

Renata's jaw twitched. A split second, and something broke in her face. "A family raised me. Taken care of by people I did not choose, but they took me in and cared for me. Gabriella… was not part of that."

Franco broke the silence at last. "That doesn't mean you weren't part of her."

Renata's eyes cut through to him, and now the air was truly charged. "You always speak in riddles, or is that just your high and mighty lifestyle talking?" Renata might be young, but she was no dummy. And she recognized Franco when she saw him. After all, he was a national hero after the 2023 Ryder Cup celebrations in Rome. She liked the game.

"Little of both." Franco grinned, internally amused and wondering how this young beauty already recognized him.

Not a single person in the room moved. Not a single blink was offered.

"We're staying in Siena a few days," Gio said. "If you want to talk, we are at the Grand Siena. I'll leave you my cell." Renata gave a single nod, cool as ice, then warm as fire. "Sure. Of course."

He paused at the door. "Gabby wasn't the kind of person to leave loose ends. I'm starting to think maybe neither are you."

She didn't say anything.

Franco slapped him on the back as they hit the street. "That went well."

"She didn't slam the door."

"High bar, my friend."

Chapter 10

Meatballs in the Sauce

The Siena sun was beating on the hot, dry afternoon when Gio and Franco slid into a seat at a small bar just off the quieter end of Via di Città. A proper aperitivo spot, the kind that didn't cater to tourists, where the afternoon spritz came bitter and the olives came with a story.

Franco leaned in. "So, tell me what you're thinking?"

Gio stirred the ice in his Negroni. "She's not ready. And I don't want to chase her."

"You always did have a soft spot for complicated women."

"Yeah, well. Chasing's what got me in trouble the first time."

Franco let that hang for a second, then shrugged. "So what's the play?"

"I'll ask her to meet me for lunch. No pressure. Quiet place. Baccon del Prete, over on Via San Pietro, away from the square."

"That little courtyard trattoria?"

"Yeah. Best pici pasta in the city. No tourists, no noise. She can say no. Or not show up. Her call."

Franco grinned. "Order some good wine."

"She can select for herself. I'm not running a sales pitch here."

Franco leaned back, taking in the street as only a celebrity could do. "While you wait for the lady, I will check in with a few friends. The Palio's coming up. Some of the Contrade captains owe me drinks."

"You're looking to gamble, aren't you?"

"Only on you, amico."

Gio cracked a small smile, the first real one all day. "Keep your bets light. You know how Siena holds a grudge."

Franco raised his glass. "We'll both keep it light. For now."

They sat in easy silence, the kind that fit their friendship. Just two men chasing down the next right thing in a country that didn't let go of its past or stories.

Chapter 11

A Call to the Table

Two mornings later, Gio sat at a small café near the Duomo, shooting his espresso straight, no sugar. The city moved around him, slow but deliberate as any typical day in the heart of Tuscany.

Siena was a UNESCO World Heritage site and one of the best-preserved medieval towns in all of Italy. The *citta* could overwhelm a stranger with its maze of taller buildings and tiny alleyways. Its intimidation forced many tourists to seek the comfort and open space of the grand Piazza and Gothic Duomo.

As a writer and storyteller, Siena was Gio's kind of place. Hidden in the Contrade were the poetic words and directional avenues for the next great adventure, one more personal than even his own life story.

No word yet from Renata. He didn't expect one, quickly. Gio understood how some people ran from loose ends; he'd done it plenty of times himself when the heat intensified, or the walls closed in.

Just then, his phone buzzed.

A short message…Baccon del Prete. Today. 12:15 sharp. I know the owner.

No name. No greeting.

He smiled. "Gabby, you're still pulling strings," he muttered to himself.

Chapter 12

Gabby Redux

Baccon del Prete was quiet; the lunchtime rush was still half an hour away. Gio picked the corner table just off the courtyard, the one with the cracked terracotta tiles and the crooked chair... Less chance of eavesdropping.

Renata arrived right on time, tight jeans, no frills, dark hair pulled back. She was young, yet totally mature beyond her 24 years, and her icy blue eyes still hit him hard. Again, he didn't let it show.

"You're early," she said as she sat.

"Habit," Gio replied. "Places like this, you show up late, you get stuck with the tourist wine."

"Smart," she said, flagging down the waiter without considering a menu. "Pici cacio e pepe. Vino rosso della casa."

"You've been here before."

"A few times. I don't like places that try too hard."

Gio grinned a little while ordering his pasta with pesto. "You don't either, huh?"

She almost smiled. Almost.

They eased into a rhythm with slow, unassuming talk. About the piazza, about the Palio, about how Siena pretended to be big but everyone knew everyone's story.

"So why'd you come looking for me?" she finally asked, setting her glass down.

"Because Gabby told me to."

"That's it? You just… listen to people who aren't here anymore?"

"Sometimes the ones who aren't here speak the loudest."

She studied him. "You don't talk like a guy who stays in one place."

"I didn't," Gio admitted. "Did a lot of running. This place slowed me down."

"Because of her?"

"Yeah. Because of her."

Renata twirled her pasta, then paused. "You and Gabby…you were what, lovers? Family?"

"Both."

"She ever tell you about me?"

"Not a word. That's the kicker. I found out through the letter."

"And you still came."

"She said you'd be waiting."

Renata looked off toward the far end of the courtyard. "I wasn't."

"That's what you keep saying."

"You close with your family?" she asked suddenly, flipping the script.

"Not until recently. My mother and I, let's just say we're figuring it out."

Renata smirked, thinking kindred spirits. "Guess we both know how to keep people at arm's length."

"That's one thing I know how to do."

She sipped her wine, watching him. "And what's the thing you don't know how to do?"

Gio cracked a slight grin. "Stay put."

"That's why you're still here, huh? Trying to prove yourself wrong?"

"Something like that."

They continued eating without forcing more talk. Gio let the next question hang inside for a while before letting it out.

"You know," he said, careful now, "it's not just Gabby I don't know everything about. I don't know anything about…the other side of your story."

Renata's fork paused mid-air. "You mean him."

"I don't even know his name."

"You didn't ask Antoinette?"

"She wouldn't tell me."

Renata leaned back. "People in Florence used to say he ran gold. Ponte Vecchio. Old network."

"Have you ever met him?"

"Not really. Not properly."

"You ever want to?"

She looked him dead in the eye. "What would be the point?"

"Sometimes people need to know where the cracks are."

Renata gave a slow nod, like maybe that made sense.

"Look," Gio said, "I'm not here to fix anything. I don't even know what there is to fix. But if you want to figure this out, I'm here to help. It was Gabby's wish."

Gio wanted to share with Renata all about La Terre Felice, how it could be the tangible connection to her birth mother and family. But he held off for now. All in time, as he started to put the pieces together for this unfolding story.

"You'll be close by?"

"Of course, he said."

She pulled a folded note from her bag and slid it across the table. "His name. That's all I have. You'll know where to look."

He pocketed it. "Thanks."

"I'm not doing this for him."

"Neither am I."

She stood. "You know where to find me if you need me."

Gio watched her go, her dark hair catching the sunlight just enough to make his chest tighten.

Franco would've called it fate. Gio just stared, dumbfounded.

Chapter 13

Franco's Siena Connections

Franco liked Siena, too. It was just the right size for a guy like him. Big enough to disappear, small enough that the right bartender could tell you who everyone was sleeping with.

He crossed into the Torre district, where the alleyways curved like secrets, and ducked into Bar Tino, one of his old haunts. He used to pass time here on tour breaks early in his career, nursing espresso and eavesdropping on the city's heartbeat.

Lorenzo, the owner, didn't miss a beat when Franco slid onto a stool.

"Reno, the Italian celebrity," Lorenzo said, wiping down the counter.

Franco grinned. "Good to see you, my friend."

"Negroni?"

"Always."

The clink of ice, the slow pour, the ritual. Franco took his first sip, savoring the sharp bite of the Campari.

"So, what brings you back?" Lorenzo asked, sliding a bowl of almonds across.

"Business. Siena's Palio is soon. Figured I'd get a bead on who's backing who this year."

Lorenzo smirked. "Always the gambler."

Franco shrugged. "A man's gotta have his hobbies."

They talked horses, rivalries, and how this year's race would be nastier than the last. The usual.

But then Lorenzo leaned in, dropping his voice. "You know who's back in the game?"

"Who?"

"Some of the old gold runners. Florence boys. Used to work the Ponte Vecchio. Rumor is that one of their lieutenants resurfaced in Siena. Not Mazocca, he's been put away for a long time, but tied to him. Quiet now but poking around."

Florence and Siena have long histories and even longer rivalries dating back to the Middle Ages. Primarily driven by political, economic, and cultural control, Florence was seen as the dominant republic, while Siena fought for independence and governance. Today, it continues with Florence holding onto a renowned Renaissance spirit, and Siena boasting its unique style. The Palio is a great example that showcases Siena's pride and independence.

Franco straightened a little. "Florence gold trade? That's old money. I thought that network dried up."

"Maybe it did. Maybe it didn't. Names don't travel on paper, Franco. They travel in whispers."

"Who's whispering?"

Lorenzo shrugged. "You didn't hear it from me."

Franco tossed back the last of his drink. "I never do."

Lorenzo tapped the counter with a knowing grin. "You should tell your friend Marzo to keep his head up. Siena's not always the sleepy village he thinks it is."

"Gio knows," Franco said, standing. "He's just stubborn enough to keep walking toward the fire anyway."

As Franco moved outside and into the afternoon sun, making way to his meetup with Gio, he knew two things:

One, he owed Lorenzo another drink soon.

Two, Gio's world was about to get messier, and probably sooner than he thought.

Chapter 14

Strategy as Recipe

The streets around the square were thinning as the shops closed for the usual afternoon snooze. Siena had that way about it. Never in a rush, but never asleep either.

Franco found Gio where he figured he'd be, leaning against a stone wall near the square, watching the afternoon unfold like he was waiting for something to chase him.

"You look like a man who just missed his train," Franco said, falling in step.

"Maybe I did," Gio replied without moving. "What'd you find?"

Franco motioned toward a café he liked, Bar Gallo Nero, small, quiet, no tourists. Perfect for a private talk.

They ordered spritzes.

Franco wasted no time. "The Palio is heating up. Districts are getting cutthroat. But that's just the surface noise."

Gio gave him a look. *"Subito al punto."*

Franco leaned forward. "The old Florence gold trade, people still talk like it's dead. It's not. Some of Mazocca's past contacts are back sniffing around. Not out in the open but connected."

"Renata's father?"

Franco shrugged, letting the possibility hang. "Could be. I didn't get a name. But Lorenzo said some Florence boys are quietly poking into Siena. And Gabby's time in Florence? That wasn't just school. She was also avoiding something."

Gio's jaw tightened. "She never told me."

Franco stirred the ice in his glass. "Maybe she wanted to. Maybe she thought you'd keep running."

The jab landed, but Gio didn't push back.

"Renata slipped me the name, Santino Buca, her father," Gio said. "You think Renata's the one who sent the letter?" *Gio wanted to hear himself say it aloud.*

Franco smiled but didn't answer directly. "Feels like something Gabby would put in motion. Like a final test."

"You're guessing."

"Sure. But you're the story guy. When's the last time life handed you this neat of a headline?"

Gio smirked despite himself. "Never."

They sipped in silence, letting the buzz of the narrow street fill the gaps.

"She'll find me if she wants to," Gio said finally.

Franco nodded. "Sharing the name with you, I'd bet she already has."

Gio let that sit, then waved for the check.

"We head back tomorrow?"

"Yeah," Gio said, tossing a few bills on the table. "La Terre Felice doesn't run itself."

"Good," Franco said, standing. "I've got a few Palio bets to place anyway."

As they walked back toward the heart of Siena, Franco tossed one last comment over the side of his shoulder.

"Careful, Gio. Women with a story like Renata, and a father like Buca, don't cross your path by accident."

"Neither do friends like you," Gio shot back.

"Yeah, but I'm cheaper."

Franco's grin hung in the air as they disappeared into the Siena streets.

Chapter 15

La Terre Felice Is a Festa Dance

Antoinette had been distracted for days while the boys were gone. She was not her usual cheerful self. Everyone around her knew she was different. It was abnormal.

The crew at La Terre Felice functioned on autopilot with only light oversight. They had rhythm, and when something or someone was offbeat, they knew it.

Maria prepped the guest rooms with soft efficiency. Paolo polished the exterior courtyard, sweeping the final stray cypress needles into a tidy pile. Sofia straightened the lanterns along the gravel pathway, ensuring her eye was on the details that made this place feel like home.

Antoinette bustled in the kitchen between her chefs, her sleeves pulled up, speaking with a serene firmness as she shouted orders. They had another meal to make, another guest to greet. There was no time to let on that she was as distracted as everyone could tell.

Gio and Franco had returned to La Terre Felice from Siena as if it were business as usual.

Life on the estate didn't care if one was absent for days or months. It just kept on keeping on.

Gio found himself leaning against the kitchen doorway, watching as Antoinette effortlessly kept pace in the chaos.

"You've got this place running like a festa dance," he said.

Antoinette looked at him without expression. "It runs because we refuse to let it stop."

Franco walked past them with a smile. "Nonna's in charge! Don't let him forget that, Antoinette."

Antoinette smirked. It was the closest thing to winning she needed.

Luca and Isabella were out in the vineyard once again. Luca was showing Isabella some of the early effects that summer growth was having on some of the rows.

"See this?" Luca asked as he ran his hand across one of the young vines. "Stubborn little thing. Took it longer to take root, but now it will flourish."

Isabella crossed her arms and studied him. "You sound like the vines are human."

"They are." Luca didn't break eye contact with her. "Some of them just need a little more time."

She couldn't be sure if he was talking about her or the land, or maybe even himself. But she liked the fact that he was not quick to explain himself.

They moved in easy silence, neither one speaking nor rushing to fill the silence. Isabella had not been checking the time for days. Something about being at La Terre Felice did that to you.

Franco eventually joined Gio on the terrace as the sun had begun to dip lower.

"Feels good to be home, huh?" Franco said.

"Yeah," Gio responded, though his thoughts were still running on Siena.

Franco raised his glass to meet Gio's. "Don't sweat it. She'll call."

"She already has," Gio said quietly.

Franco could sense the note in his voice, but he let the subject drop for the time being.

Life at La Terre Felice trudged on for now.

Staff worked, guests arrived, vines grew, and the hot and dry summer continued.

But everyone knew that storms were not invited to this party. They just showed up.

Chapter 16

Fresh Herbs Add Flavor to the Sauce

With Franco leaving for a few weeks of tour golf, Gio was now preoccupied with the name Santino Buca. He found Nonna Antoinette in the kitchen garden pruning herbs, chopping fresh basil, and avoiding eye contact. It was so unlike her.

Gio leaned against the garden gate, arms crossed, eyes on her.

"Have you ever heard the name Santino Buca?"

Antoinette's knife paused mid-chop. Not long, but long enough.

"Where'd you hear that?"

"In Siena," Gio said. "I met with Renata. She handed me a note with his name. Franco also picked up information through some old contacts from Florence. His name keeps surfacing like a bad gold coin."

Antoinette resumed her chopping. "That man was trouble then. Still is."

"So Gabby knew him."

Antoinette didn't look up. "She was smart, beautiful, and sixteen. He was older. Dangerous in the way young girls find thrilling."

"She got pregnant."

Antoinette finally looked at him. "Yes."

Gio absorbed it all. He suspected as much, but hearing it—clean, direct—made the whole thing land heavier.

"Why didn't she tell me?" he asked.

"She was protecting Renata. And maybe you," Antoinette said, brushing herbs into a bowl. "Antonio and I thought it was best to keep her away at school. Santino wasn't the kind of man who wanted a family or a young pregnant girl. And he would not be the kind of father to raise a daughter gently."

"And Renata?"

"She was raised by a family in Fiesole. Good people with a loving home in a beautiful village. Gabby stayed close when she could, but never as her mother. It broke her."

Gio ran a hand through his hair. "So you all just decided to erase her?"

"She wasn't erased," Antoinette snapped. "She was shielded."

Silence stretched between them. Heart-wrenching for two people who grew so close during Gabby's illness and over the past year at La Terre Felice.

"She knows who Gabby is," Antoinette added. "She always knew. But what she knows about Santino…I can't say."

"She's asked to meet me again," he said as he turned to leave. "This time I'll ask her directly."

Antoinette didn't stop him. "Be careful what you ask, Gio. Not every answer will give you peace."

Chapter 17

A Second Meeting…Another Meal…More Intrigue

Castelnuovo Berardenga was a small commune—a village, really—southeast of Florence and a few miles east of Siena. It shares a border with the Chianti wine region of Tuscany and produces some of the region's best Sangiovese vintages.

Gio rode his Vespa to Locanda degli Ulivi, a family-run trattoria built into an olive grove outside of the village. Locals frequented the place for its privacy and the grilled pecorino, a cheese known for its pungent flavor when dipped in sweetness.

As a travel writer, Gio had been in similar situations before when a story he was working on became personal. The courtyard of the trattoria was rustic at the least. Gravel floor. One waiter. Two tables set with a view of the rolling hills of the Chianti Val d'Orcia. No music. All good.

He didn't have to wait long. Renata arrived easily, striding to the table with purpose. Her hair was pulled back, and her linen blouse had been tucked carelessly into her jeans, revealing a strong, perky view.

Gio imagined a young Gabby, but not in the obvious way. In the shape of her face. Her mystery. The storm of thought behind her eyes. And those eyes…that deep, irresistible, unmistakable blue.

"*Ciao*," she said, almost cautiously.

Gio rose to offer a handshake. "*Grazie mille* for coming."

"I wasn't sure," she replied. "But I figured Gabby wouldn't have written that letter if you weren't worth meeting again."

They sat. The waiter poured water and left them to it.

"So," she said, squeezing her hands together tightly. "What do you want to know?"

"I spoke to Antoinette," Gio said, getting straight to the point. "She filled me in on Santino Buca."

Renata's expression did not flinch. "Then I guess the mystery is off the table."

"He's still alive?"

Renata nodded. "I've never met him," she said. "Gabby made sure of that. Said he wasn't the kind of man who deserved a daughter. Last I heard, he still runs a string of shady enterprises in Florence. Jewelry. Black market metals. People disappear around him."

"She turned you over to another family."

"She gave me a real one," Renata corrected gently. "A quiet family outside of Fiesole. They had no reason to take me in except to love and protect a child. Gabby stayed as close as she could. But at a distance."

"She watched your life like it was behind glass."

Renata gave a quiet smile. "Exactly."

Gio studied her for a moment. "Did you ever resent her for that?"

Renata looked away. "I wanted to. When I was younger, yes. But she stayed connected in her own way. I had her art drawings. Letters I wasn't supposed to know were from her. She always watched like a ghost who couldn't leave the room."

Gio let that sit for a moment. "You mailed her letter to me, didn't you?"

She hesitated. "Gabby gave it to me before she passed. Said I'd know when to send it."

"Why now?"

"Because she said you needed time to stop running. And I'd know when you were still enough to listen. I am a voracious reader and aware of the publicity you received for La Terre Felice, so that told me there was a solid and consistent stewardship over the past year."

He didn't answer that right away. Just nodded slowly.

The silence stretched again.

"I don't know what Gabby wanted between us," Renata said, finally. "I'm not here to claim anything. I don't want your sympathy."

"You've got my attention," Gio said.

She allowed herself a small smirk. "Gabby always said that would be the hardest part because of your inquisitive nature."

They ordered a light lunch—tagliolini al limone—thin ribbons of fresh pasta in a light lemon cream, shaved Parmigiano melting at the edges. Renata twirled hers slowly, washing it down with a clean, citrusy Vino Bianco. In contrast, Gio ate with more purpose and at a fork-heavy pace with a rugged glass of dry Chianti.

Besides his ability to dig into and craft a story, Gio had another claim to fame when it came to food. He let his stomach drive his instinct and rarely ordered a bad meal off a menu.

The conversation was lighter: Florence, books, the strange quiet of a hot Tuscan summer, and the tension of living with a name that carried a weight you didn't choose.

The thread between them pulled tighter. Yet the air never lost its intrigue. Despite Gio's reputation, it wasn't romantic. It was something more fragile: two people unsure of what connected them now that the woman who once tethered them both was gone.

As they stood to leave, Gio said, "Renata, would you like to see La Terre Felice?"

"I've thought about it every day since Gabby died," Renata said. "I just didn't want to show up unannounced."

Renata continued to look at Gio for a long while. "But, yes, I would like that very much."

Chapter 18

Antoinette Shares an Introductory Recipe

Gio leaned against the curved window of his studio, which faced a courtyard. It was late afternoon. The agriturismo was as it normally was on such a day: locals returning from a day of touring the region and now searching for their spritzes; the clang of glasses and high noise of voices and laughter; and the sounds of Antoinette's kitchen at work.

He didn't turn when he heard the door open.

Antoinette entered without waiting to be invited. "You haven't been out of this room all day," she observed.

Gio sniffed through his nose. "Trying to figure out Siena. And you."

She seated herself across Gio's messy writing desk. "Well, I deserve that."

"I didn't go looking for secrets," Gio said. "But I do know the business of investigation. Secrets have a way of catching you in the face when you least expect them."

Antoinette remained silent for a moment. She looked older in the sunlight—frayed, but not frail.

"Gabby made choices," she said at last. "Choices that I didn't agree with at first. But she thought it was right. For Renata. For all of us."

"You should have told me," Gio said, voice thick. "After she died. Before the letter. Before any of this."

"I almost did," she admitted. "But then I'd see the way you looked at her chair by the fireplace, and I couldn't do it. You weren't ready."

"I know it was hard for you to believe sometimes, but she was my life. And you took part of her from me."

Antoinette nodded. "I did. And I'm sorry."

The two of them sat in silence for a moment. Gio heard staff down in the piazza chuckle as a tray was dropped.

"She's coming here," Gio said, at last turning to face Antoinette. "Renata. We've decided to meet again. At La Terre Felice. She should see it."

Antoinette nodded once more. "Then we should prepare the staff. Be honest with them but remind them to be discreet. Franco's away golfing, so this one is on you and me."

Gio sat down in the chair at his desk and rubbed his eyes. "And when Franco gets back, he and I are going to Florence. I want to know what Santino Buca's angle is, if he's still alive, and if he has any legal means to try to get to Renata. Or to this place."

"I always worried he'd come sniffing around," Antoinette said. "He never stopped being a threat. That's why Gabby did what she did."

Gio looked out the window once more. "You really think she has a claim?"

Antoinette paused. "Not today. But maybe one day. Gabby wanted her to choose this life, not have it forced on her. If she ever shares in La Terre Felice, it should be given to her by us. Not by lawyers. And certainly not by Santino."

Gio slowly nodded. "Then we do this right. Carefully. And together."

"*Concordata*," Antoinette agreed.

Chapter 19

A Table of Their Own

On the days without guests on the estate, the courtyard at La Terre Felice was used as a workspace. As if the vineyard needed a place to catch its breath when it was empty.

A long table had been dragged out under the canopy of trees in the back of the main farmhouse, and chairs had been stolen from every room and kitchen in the compound. No refined service, no linen tablecloths, just family-style food, carafes of wine, and the kind of honest conversation that reminded them all why they were doing this.

Antoinette's staff prepared bowls of pici tangled with lemon zest and fresh ricotta. Grilled zucchini and eggplant glistened with olive oil. Roasted chicken with rosemary and garlic was tucked beside torn loaves of crusty Tuscan bread. Antoinette also baked a crostata with figs and honey for dessert later, but it was already sitting in the middle of the table as a lure.

Gio leaned back in his chair, turning his wine glass in his hand slowly as he watched the people around him: Maria cracking a joke that made Paolo nearly choke on his Chianti; Sofia laughing as she dabbed olive oil from her chin with the back of her hand; Luca sawing meat from the bone and holding it out to Isabella like a gentleman thief. Gio's mother took it from him with a smirk and a wink.

These were the people who made La Terre Felice work. The ones who showed up on the hard days and stayed for the better ones. Today, Gio had to tell them something that would change the rhythm of this place yet again. And he wasn't sure how they would take it.

He tapped his glass gently with the edge of his fork. A gentle chime rose over the low hum of conversation.

"*Posso?*" Gio asked. *May I?*

The table quieted. Some people leaned forward. Antoinette set her napkin down and met his eye with a subtle nod.

"*Grazie,*" Gio began. "We wanted today to be a thank you. For your hard work. For holding this place steady when it felt like the world was spinning without Gabby here to guide it. I am grateful to all of you. To my mother, to my friends, to my family; not all by blood, but by choice."

He paused, letting his words sink in.

"But there's one more thing we need to talk about. Something...unexpected. Something Gabby never told most of us."

A hush.

Gio looked to Antoinette, who folded her hands in her lap. "Go on," she whispered. "It's time."

He took a breath. "Gabby had a daughter. Her name is Renata. She's twenty-four now, and she's coming here soon."

There was silence at first. Forks stilled, wine glasses stopped in midair.

Maria and Luca exchanged a look. Quiet. Knowing.

"You knew?" Paolo asked, turning to face them.

Maria nodded slowly. "Gabby told us years ago. But only once. She made us promise not to say a word unless she did."

Isabella's hand went to her chest. "Madonna," she breathed. "Gabriella was just a young girl herself when she would've had her."

"She was," Antoinette said softly. "It wasn't the right time. And she thought...for a while, she thought giving Renata another kind of life was the better choice."

Sofia wiped at her eyes. "So why now?"

"She wrote me a letter," Gio said. "Before she died. She asked Renata to come here. To see what we built. To find her truth. And maybe, to find us."

No one said a word.

"She looks like Gabby," he added. "But lighter somehow. She has her eyes – that same impossible blue. And she carries a quiet sadness, like she's been holding her breath her whole life."

He was standing now, lifting his glass.

"I don't know what Renata's place here is yet. But I know Gabby wanted her to have a chance to find it. I ask that you all welcome and get to know her. She is part of this family, and Gabby's wish is for her to learn about La Terre Felice."

Maria rose with him, raising her glass. "To Renata," she said. "And to Gabby, who trusted us to carry on."

And just like that, the courtyard filled once more; not just with food, sun, and laughter, but with the whisper of another chapter beginning for the agriturismo.

Chapter 20

Shifting Light at La Terre Felice

The lunch feast had ended. The courtyard was empty and still bore the scent of roasted garlic and rosemary. Bottles of empty wine rested on the table where they had been served, and napkins—now crumpled like parchment paper—sat next to half-eaten plates of Antoinette's crostata and biscotti.

Inside, the kitchen was quiet, too. Antoinette lingered wordlessly, a hand resting lightly on the picture frame near the spice rack. A picture of Gabby in flour, her cheeks and a curl of hair, in mid-laugh. Antoinette did not talk to it. Oh, she wanted to, so many times. She walked more slowly around it now, and she caught her breath as if she would.

She set her hands on the counter, leaning over the empty sink. "Domani," she murmured. "Tomorrow. She comes tomorrow."

Outside, Gio walked the length of the lower vineyard with a small journal in his hand. His notes had become half-poem, half-confession. He knew it. Gabby would tease him for it. He smiled at the memory, and he stopped mid-path to scrawl something on a page.

She has her mother's eyes. But she doesn't look for me with them.
She walks into a life I've already fucked up more than once.
How do you say 'welcome home' to someone who doesn't know it is?

He closed the notebook and looked back toward the villa, back toward the olive trees that overhung the terrace. The sun was sliding behind them. Another glorious Tuscan evening had arrived.

Isabella and Luca moved slowly in the east garden, between rows of tomato and zucchini plants. She chided him for overwatering again.

"Mamma mia, it's not a swimming pool, Luca."

He raised an eyebrow. "It's *amore*. My zucchinis are affectionate."

She shook her head and then laughed. For real this time. He handed her a tomato, one that had ripened to a bright red. And for a second, their hands touched and lingered.

Something was cooking…and more than a juicy tomato.

Upstairs, in the guestroom that Renata would be moving into the next day, a fresh set of linens lay folded at the foot of the bed. A vase of white flowers stood on the desk, one that Maria had set down.

Downstairs, Antoinette came from the kitchen and gave a quiet glance to Gio, who had moved to stand in the open frame of the archway.

"She deserves to see the real place," Gio said.

"She will," Antoinette responded.

"Do you think she'll stay?"

Antoinette did not answer at once. She watched the length of the property as shadows grew longer and evening drew close.

"She might. But not for us. Not yet."

Gio nodded.

Then, almost as an afterthought, he asked, "Do you think Gabby would be proud of us?"

Antoinette turned, and she ran her hands over her apron, cleaning them. She did not smile, but her eyes crinkled.

"She already was. The night before she died. She said, 'They'll know what to do.'"

Gio looked down at the journal in his hand. He tapped the edge with his fingers.

Tomorrow, Renata will come. And with her, the beginning of everything.

Chapter 21

Renata…Oh, Those Tuscan Blues!

The day of Renata's arrival was hot and dry; an all-too-common occurrence that was beginning to worry the staff at the agriturismo. The tall cypress trees that lined the property as columns at the entrances to the valleys swayed gently in the afternoon breeze, ushering her into the property as her car descended from the narrow provincial road onto the gravel drive leading to La Terre Felice.

Renata pulled to a stop in front of the main courtyard, shaded by ancient olive trees. She opened her door cautiously, taking in slow breaths and surveying the grounds with its terra-cotta tiles sun-bleached in places, vines heavy with summer growth, a wooden sign with the name in a hand-painted script: *La Terre Felice*.

"Renata?"

She looked up to see a tall woman emerging from the shadow of a fig tree. Linen apron. Gold earrings. Hair back in a loose bun. Before she even smiled, her voice was warm.

Antoinette's maternal instincts kicked in. "Welcome," she said, pulling Renata into a quick hug that somehow felt earned. Pulling back a step, she observed Gabby's daughter: the dark hair, her posture, the easy grace, and most of all, her eyes: the same shade of blue that had once belonged to her daughter.

It was at that moment that Gio appeared, having emerged from the front of the main house. He met her eyes and looked, unflinchingly, at her for a moment. Maybe he was looking through her, searching. The moment they shared was wordless, but there was something between them. A stirring of the air, a heartbeat that seemed to slow.

He then gave his usual sly little smile. Polite. Complex. "You found us," he said.

"I did." Renata swallowed the lump in her throat. "It's...it's so much."

"Come," Antoinette said. "Let's get you inside. You've driven enough for the day."

A young employee emerged from the kitchen to collect Renata's luggage and carry it upstairs. Gio offered to help with the bags, but she waved him off with a soft "let her arrive."

The interior of the house was pleasantly cool. The air smelled strongly of lemon and basil. The young woman followed Antoinette into the airy salon just off the kitchen. A small table had been prepared with a glass of chilled peach tea, a few homemade almond biscotti, and a linen napkin embroidered with olive branches.

"Something to keep your hunger at bay." Antoinette placed her hand on Renata's shoulder. "You'll have all the time in the world to explore this place. But first, let's sit."

Renata sipped slowly, taking in the rustic stone walls, the warm afternoon light as it angled through the windows, and the distant sound of children's laughter from the kitchen garden.

"If you're ready, your room is prepared," Antoinette said. "No need to rush, of course."

Gio had not said much. He'd lingered in the doorway for a moment, and after a slight nod, he headed back outside.

She remained seated for a few minutes more, savoring the cool drink, letting her breathing and her emotions finally synchronize with her body.

She was here. Really here.

And soon, she would walk through that door into the life that may have always been hers.

Renata caught the brief awkwardness of the encounter. No one knew what to do. She was a stranger in the family. As she sat and rested, she couldn't help but feel that she belonged. Gabby was spiritually everywhere at La Terre Felice.

Chapter 22

The New Ingredient for La Terre Felice

Renata left the guesthouse wearing a clean linen blouse, her hair loosely bound back, her shoulders relaxed. The courtyard was draped in sunlight, filtered through grapevines overhead. It was mostly quiet now, but for the chirping of birds and the distant hum of traffic along the coastal road.

Antoinette leaned casually against the entrance to the kitchen garden. "Better?" she asked with a warm smile.

"Much," Renata said. "I took your advice and drank some lemon water in my room. It was perfect. And this place...it's already better than I imagined."

Gio was stacking wine crates against the stone retaining wall near the garden. He tilted his head at her and offered a perfunctory nod. "You'll love it when Luca shows you. He'll have you swooning before you've seen it all."

"Luca?"

As if on cue, Luca strode out from behind a row of sunflowers, sleeves rolled up and skin tanned and dusted with dirt. He moved with a kind of sinewy grace. He yanked a small Parodi cigar from behind one ear and lit it with a match he flicked from his boot sole.

"I'm Luca," he said, puffing it as he smiled. "Tour guide, unofficial historian…and the voice of reason when Gio tries to channel his inner tourist."

Renata laughed. "Lead on then."

Walking the gravel path that curved along the edge of the villa, Renata took it all in. To her right were rows of cottages, their stone walls and terra-cotta roofs barely visible through the overgrown gardens that seemed to sprout organically from the hillside. Charming in their own right—ivy hanging from walls, small patios or porticos overhung by pergolas—there was a feeling of coziness and abandon to them.

"We have people stay there," Luca said, catching her looking. "Couples. Some writers, musicians. A few celebrities looking to escape, while others never leave. Gabby had it built so that people could feel like they're staying in a village. Private enough to rest but close enough to share a bottle of wine with a stranger."

He gestured to one of the cottages, where a woman was brushing the stone stoop with a wide straw broom. She looked up as they approached and smiled at Renata, waving. "Benvenuta, cara. You must be the special guest."

"That's Maria," Luca said. "Housekeeping, unofficial matchmaker, and the one who'll slip you extra biscotti if you catch her eye."

"She already has," Renata said.

They walked past an orchard of fig trees, where a tall man in a straw hat paused to work on some irrigation lines and clip low-hanging branches. He wiped his forehead on a dirty sleeve and nodded at Luca. "Tell your friend the vines are drinking well today."

"*Grazie*, Paolo," Luca called.

"Hey," he said to Renata, "to this day, Paolo will not touch an app or a machine. He works the land the way Gabby's father did—listens to the vines, smells the dirt, adapts by instinct."

Renata stared at it all in silence, eyes wide, her chest tightening with something she couldn't yet name. Mature beyond her years, Renata knew that this was more than just a working vineyard. It was the stuff of memory and mission. But could it be something more?

They came upon a low stone wall that looked out over the valley, where green rows of vines tumbled down the hillside in a chaotic pattern, olive trees and gnarled cypress settled in like holy relics.

Gio wandered up behind them, both hands in his pockets. "That's right, Luca. Gabby built the bones of the place. But it's taken all of us to keep it alive."

They all stood there in companionable silence for a moment, taking in the view.

Renata said at last, "It's more than I imagined. There's something...living in this place."

Luca released a long stream of smoke and nodded. "Because this was built on love. And stubbornness. And maybe a little madness."

Gio's phone buzzed in his pocket. He tugged it out and read the message silently.

It was from Franco: *I've got something. Meet me in Florence next week. You'll want to see this.*

He shoved the phone back in his pocket, his brow furrowing ever so slightly.

"Everything okay?" Renata asked.

"Could be," Gio said. "Or could be the beginning of something...messy."

She looked at him, knowing there was more. He exhaled slowly, his eyes searching the vineyard behind her.

"Let's just say there are a lot of stories beneath these vines," Gio said. "Some of which are ready to be told."

Chapter 23

Gio's Sports Analogy Builds a Menu for Life

Gio had grown used to the quiet. Not silence, exactly—La Terre Felice was always alive with the workings of the agriturismo, laughter, and the hum of natural enjoyment from guests the world over. It was the kind of quiet that wrapped around you when the world finally let you breathe.

It had been three days since Renata arrived. Her presence still stirred something in him. There was an energy he felt but couldn't yet recognize.

In the early mornings, Gio rose before the sun and wandered the property. He'd take his espresso beneath the canopy, a leather-bound notebook in hand. But he wasn't journaling this time. He was following a thread. Giulio Mazocca. A name he hadn't thought about since Gabby's funeral, when the aftereffects of Mazocca's land deals had been too raw to pursue further.

He'd made a few calls. He wanted to know more about Santino Buca and his ties to Mazocca and the underground economy, well known in Central Italy. A friend at a Tuscan registry office pulled a favor. A librarian at the Florence City Archives promised a few overlooked records.

Gio knew this dance—it wasn't his first time tracing shadows through bureaucracy. But this wasn't for a magazine spread. This was personal. And in the back of his mind, always, a baseball or golf analogy.

Growing up in the States, Gio had fallen in love with baseball and the New York Yankees, not just for the game, but for the legend his grandfather passed down over bowls of pasta and homemade Chianti.

Signore Giovanni repeatedly told the story of once meeting Joe DiMaggio in the most unexpected place—a small coal town tucked in the hills of Northeast Pennsylvania. Life in that part of the Commonwealth was tough, and Giovanni spent many evenings with a group of guys who hung around the town's liveliest street corner; not much to do, but it was theirs.

There was a luncheonette close by, and one evening while stopping by, Giovanni ran into none other than the "Yankee Clipper" himself, Joe DiMaggio.

DiMaggio was god-like to Italian Americans who immigrated to the U.S. Besides the Catholic church and Sunday dinner, Joe D. was their patron saint and hero in the sporting world.

"I never asked DiMaggio why he was there," Giovanni would say, retelling his story many times. "I just wanted his signature for my own." This would become something special in the family.

Back then, nobody cared about baseball cards or collectors' value. All Giovanni had in his wallet was a business card from a local house painter. DiMaggio obliged and signed the card. Giovanni held onto it his entire life and passed it on to Gio before he died. Gio safely tucked it away, occasionally pulling it out for inspiration that anything is possible in sports and life.

Memorabilia aficionados say it's not worth much since it doesn't appear on a piece of baseball equipment. Yet, for Gio, that signature is as crisp today as when it was penned many years ago…and priceless in so many ways.

That story became a compass for Gio, a reminder that the extraordinary often hides in the ordinary. Now he needed another one of those moments. Maybe Florence would deliver.

Whether baseball or golf, the game was on, and this time, Gio was chasing more than a story.

Chapter 24

The City of the Medici

Florence never slept. The sun of Italy scorched Brunelleschi's Duomo in amber light, and Ghiberti's baptistry, 'Gates to Paradise' doors in reflective gold. The elaborate Duomo was a rising monument over narrow winding streets and alleyways alive with history and secrets. The air was thick with the odor of new leather from the market stalls mixed with the sharp tang of espresso and the smoky aroma of roasted chestnuts. Permeating the Renaissance air were the ghosts of the Medici.

Tourists jostled each other in Piazza del Duomo, some to and from the Uffizi to gawk at Botticelli's work, others drawn to the Galleria dell'Accademia to stand beneath Michelangelo's David, a spectacular, 17-foot-tall carved masterpiece whose oversized hands and feet seemed to command courage and provide balance beyond the years.

Gio and Franco stood by Piazza della Repubblica, Gio nursing a slow espresso, while Franco sported shades and gazed at the throngs, half-hidden in the DP Tour hoodie, like a local.

"You look like a guy scouting the joint for a museum robbery," Franco joked, thumping Gio's back.

"Or worse," Gio shrugged.

They wandered together through cobbled streets, Gio half-smirking as Franco gestured wildly, finally stopping on the Arno near Ponte Vecchio, the famed old bridge.

Sunlight bounced off the medieval shops lining the crossing. There were gold dealers, watchmakers, family jewelry stores that had been around for generations, and more gold dealers. The bridge was not just a romantic must-see for lovers in the city. It had been the home of much power and money from Florence's gold trade and was still, to a large degree, in many ways.

Gio looked across the Arno, drawing invisible lines between then and now.

"This bridge," Gio started, low, "used to be where all the butchers and fishmongers did their work. The Medici scrubbed the streets of blood and blood money and turned the bridge into a showcase of gold. Forced the idea of beauty over murder. And now it's still about control."

Franco arched an eyebrow. "And Buca?"

"The Buca family has ties back to Santorini and the sea, but they came from more than that. My guess is he's been here before. Buca's not just playing with wine as a hustle. Buca's playing with legacy… and silence. The Ponte Vecchio is just the beginning."

Gio moved them to a quiet wine bar a few streets off Via del Giglio, and they ordered Negronis and settled on the shaded terrace of the indoor-outdoor place.

"So, I checked out the name quietly," Gio started, tracing the route of his recent day. "Santino Buca."

"Go on."

"I used some old business filings and land deeds. He and his family have roots in Bolgheri, which is a prime area for wine, but also, there's a Florence-based company in logistics for food and wine export. Surface is clean, but all the undercurrents are muddy. And do you know what else? Mazocca's name appears more than a few times in the run-up."

Franco leaned in, dark eyes on Gio's face. "Buca isn't some street thug. He's a businessman with a lot of muscle behind him, and he's not afraid to use it. Plus, he is aware of his heritage and the significance of his family name. Memory."

Before Gio could respond, a woman passed through the square, a crimson dress sliding against her form and whipping in the open air as if it were part of some magical chase through the annals of time. She stopped before Gio and Franco with a hush of wind, a bold woman in full control of her body and mind.

Valentina. Valentina Mazocca.

Valentina was a seductress. Little did Gio know when he first met her at the 2023 Ryder Cup in Rome, how close he would come to losing the agriturismo for Gabby and the Rosetti family, because of his indiscretions. Valentina oozed sexual heat. Gio couldn't resist. So, Valentina and her father, Guilio Mazocca, took advantage of that weakness to attempt to steal La Terre Felice. Thanks to Franco, the boys teamed up to win it back in a golf hustle while Gio's writing exposed Mazocca's illegal business dealings. He was then sent to prison for a long time.

The tightly packed, yet sultry Valentina slid sunglasses down the bridge of her nose, the afternoon sun gleaming in her dark hair as the curls floated on a breeze. "Ciao, Gio. Still a ghost?" The smoky come-hither tone she used on all her victims.

Franco sucked air through clenched teeth. "Jesus Christ!"

Gio froze.

"What the actual fuck are you doing here, Valentina?" Gio stormed forward with every fiber of his body ready to crush and overpower this femme fatale, but she cut across him with a lunge and smirked in his direction.

Turning to Franco, Valentina shifted her hips. "And you're still breaking hearts and greens, *campione*?"

Franco gave an affirmative nod and a blink.

She grinned with that dastardly little mouth of hers. "I heard Florence is gorgeous this time of year…and I thought you two might want to know a little bit more about Santino Buca. You're in luck. I'm here to help. My father will be in prison for a very long time. He's been cut off. Dead end. But Buca? Buca's in town."

Gio felt it as soon as she spoke, despite every instinct in his body screaming the whole truth and nothing but the truth, she was trouble. The pull of Valentina. "Why help us?"

"Because you're not the only ones in trouble. I know where he'll be tomorrow afternoon——a *buchette del vino* near Borgo degli Albizi. The original wine windows. He likes to be on time. You should be there, maybe just before three."

Valentina turned from them and began to weave through the gathering street crowds, eventually disappearing into the canyon of Florence streets. Gio and Franco stared at each other before Franco focused back on Gio.

"You believe her?"

"I believe she knows something." Gio met Franco's eyes head-on, before slipping out of focus. "But we go in eyes wide open, Franco. She could be pulling strings to have us killed."

As the day waned, they made their way back to the Arno. The Ponte Vecchio was awash in gold from the slowly setting sun. Tourists in droves snapped photos like they were religious experiences, lovers kissed and pressed against the marble railings, and those in the know wondered what secrets still lay undisturbed deep below in the foundations and stones.

Gio thought of the story that was passed to him repeatedly by his grandfather...DiMaggio, the saint. A fabled tale of time, place, and everything caught between an accidental encounter outside a small Pennsylvania town and the message beyond baseball.

Sipping his Negroni, Gio recalled his grandfather's words: "Keep your eye on the ball. Everything else is noise."

He glanced at Franco. "We're about to step inside the ropes. Time to focus."

Franco smirked. "Game on."

Chapter 25

The Florence Wine Window Meeting

The wine windows of Florence were part of its history, but they were also participants in the new world. They were of the culture of the merchant, the one always on the edge of innovation and invention.

They were old. As old as the 17th century, and new markets in Europe, which, at the time, had rewritten the map, and ruined business trade in ways that had made Florence so wealthy and powerful in the Renaissance years.

They were small hatches cut through the side of a building for noble families to sell their wine, often discreetly and privately, safely through plagues or political instability or to avoid taxes...just like those not-so-discreet, under-the-table deals made everywhere today.

Now restored like quaint novelties, some of the windows in the Arno and beyond still worked. A wine window was, in its time, a functional, discreetly charming hutch where people served wine and whispers in equal measure. The windows were small arched cuttings with wooden doors. Their importance and notoriety were built during the plagues in Europe, and more recently through the COVID-19 pandemic that ravaged Italy, all part of a medical history relevance.

Florence had always been a city of secrets, but few had been hidden as conspicuously as in the walls of Renaissance palazzi in the form of the buchette del vino.

The chosen meeting place was one such window set into the thick stone wall of a nondescript building near the Ponte Vecchio. It was, of course, Valentina's decision. She had insisted on it, claimed it would be discreet, neutral, and lost amongst tourists who were intent on eating, drinking, or sightseeing.

As Gio and Franco approached the location for the meeting with Buca, Gio said, "I have my doubts about this mio amico. If the past has taught me anything, it's that Valentina does nothing without a deeper agenda."

"Her deeper agenda might be you this time, paisan," said Franco.

The air was hot in the afternoon, the stones of the city still burning with the sun's rays and holding on like old statues waiting for another life. They were the first to arrive, dressed in neutrals. No camera, no notebook. They'd blend in, watch. From their location, the Ponte Vecchio was in the distance. The shops glimmered in gold, old world and ever ready to remind everyone who would listen of Florence's history of craft and commerce…and greed.

Santino Buca was less subtle in his arrival. He was broader than Gio expected, but not much taller. His face was lined from years in the Italian sun, too much sun, and his tailored jacket did little to disguise the dirt underneath. He wore a smile, but not one that reached his eyes.

"Signor Marzo," he said with false warmth, and not looking to speak to Franco. "What a pleasure to finally meet the man who holds my daughter's fate in his hands."

Gio didn't extend his hand. "Let's not pretend this is an occasion for pleasantries."

Valentina stepped out of the shadows, casually leaning against the wall at the base of the window with studied nonchalance. She nodded at the small wooden shutter. "They'll bring out a bottle. Chianti, of course. You can both drink while you talk."

A hand appeared through the open window and pushed a carafe and two glasses across before it closed again, like the door to the vault of a secret chef preparing maritozzi pastry.

They drank. Santino took only a sip, less than a sip, before beginning his case.

"Renata," he began, slowly, "is blood. My blood. A family may have raised her after Gabriella gave birth, but her legacy, your precious La Terre Felice, is on shaky ground if her lineage is not properly recognized." He took a swallow of wine. "I am not here to be your enemy, Giovanni. I wish to be fair. To take what is owed. A share, modest, perhaps. A say in the estate's future. For her sake."

Gio placed his glass back on the cobblestone. "Don't pretend this is about Renata. You abandoned her. Gabby made sure that she never needed you, and she was right. You are not entitled to anything. Not land. Not legacy. Not even thanks."

Santino's eyes narrowed. "Careful, *ragazzo*. The world is full of stories. Stories that end badly if people hold on too tightly."

Gio stood up evenly. "Tell your story. But know that this is not yours. La Terre Felice is not for your coveting. Legally and by right of will. It was built by the Rosetti family with blood and sweat, and love. And integrity. All of which you've shown none."

Valentina remained silent, as did Franco, watching the two with unreadable expressions.

As Gio turned to leave, Santino called to him. "She'll come looking for answers. Some day. And when she does, I'll be waiting."

Gio didn't turn. "She already found them. And she knows who she is."

Gio and Franco walked away, the late sun throwing long shadows against the river's floodlit canal. Florence had seen power handed down and stolen for generations. It had been the quiet witness of a trade built and lost for time immemorial. But not this time. Not today.

Chapter 26

The Watcher in Florence

Florence had never been a museum city to Luca.

There were shadows and memories. Shadows that Luca had never discussed at La Terre Felice with anyone. Least of all, with Antoinette.

And that, of course, had been the whole point of her sending him. "Keep an eye on Gio," she'd said, "but more importantly…keep an eye on who keeps an eye on him."

Luca hadn't been sent to Florence by Antoinette because she distrusted Gio. On the contrary, she trusted Luca's eyes more than anyone else's. Luca had lived another life before La Terre Felice, a life that was buried under decades of secrets.

Luca had been an intelligence operative in the 1980s, in the days when Italy burned with political chaos. A time when the country's underground was used to channel money, men, and arms to every conspiracy, every faction, every cause, violent or otherwise. Luca had seen the faces of the men who lived in the cracks between politics, wealth, and power when the very soul of the country was up for sale.

A decade later, the lira, Italy's currency, was on its deathbed, as the country adopted common market economic concepts and introduced the Euro. The chaos of currency made gold and its trade even more visible, more valuable, and far deadlier for the uninitiated.

Luca was always at a remove, a step behind and easy in his movements, another older Italian wandering the loggias. But his eyes were never at rest for long. Never, for the familiar. He had been trained to see those faces long ago.

And now, all these years later, Luca saw one of those faces again.

On the other side of the Arno River, leaning against a shuttered shop front, was Santino Buca. He was fat now. But the essential element of the man had not changed. He was still that same hard-edged presence, inquisitive and calculating, and never lingering without purpose.

For a heartbeat, their eyes met. Buca did not blink. His lips twisted slightly. Acknowledgement. Recognition.

Amusement, perhaps. The kind of look professionals shared when both knew they had just been seen.

Luca felt his chest tighten, but his face remained unchanged. He turned towards the Ponte Vecchio, pretending to take an interest in the tourists with their cameras and poses. He glanced back and Buca was gone, melted into the crowd as though he had never been there at all.

But Luca knew better. Florence was reminding him that the past did not stay buried. And if Santino Buca was back, Gio was already walking with dangerous company, with or without his knowledge.

Chapter 27

Truth Recipe, Warnings & Valentina

The city of Di Medici could charm a man with ease without even trying. Franco and Gio found a trattoria down an alley near the Piazza della Signoria, where the music played and families picnicked. The taverna was the kind where the waiters didn't give you a menu because the dishes were at the whim of the kitchen.

The two friends ate and drank between a bottle of Brunello and plates of bistecca, laughing and teasing each other as they finally began to relax after the hectic few weeks. Franco and Gio were about to get up to go when the golf pro pushed his chair into Gio's.

"*Paisan*, I am going to say this one time—you watch your back. You know that woman is poison. You know it, and I know it. Is she beautiful? Check. Tempting? Check.

Trouble? Big check." Franco's voice was sharper than the rest of the conversation.

Gio smirked, swirling his glass. "You sound like my conscience."

"I'm being dead serious," Franco snapped. "One night with that woman is never just one night. Do you think you can only have one hot hookup with her? You must be kidding. Don't mistake heat for trust."

Gio opened his mouth to reply, but before he could get the words out, there was a shift in the trattoria. She was there. Valentina. Wearing a dark outfit with her hair down, she walked through the door as if she owned the place. Her eyes went right to Gio as if she had never left. Her eyes were as deep as the style. Gio felt the blood rush to his head.

"Case in point," Franco hissed under his breath. "Don't say I didn't warn you."

She stepped closer, lowering her voice: "You're chasing a ghost, Gio. Renata's father is far more dangerous than you realize. And if you want to protect La Terre Felice, you're going to need me."

The air was electric. As much as Gio wanted to walk away, he knew he couldn't.

A few hours later, after too much wine, too many glances, and Franco storming out with a final toss of his head, Gio found himself being led up through the cobbled streets of Florence by the scent of her perfume. Valentina led him as a flame would lure a moth, through an open door and up into a private apartment. The room had a balcony, too.

Valentina's apartment looked over the Arno. There were candles lit, and the curtains were drawn back from the cracked-open window. The breeze from the Arno moved through the room, causing the candles to flicker. But Gio barely noticed. As soon as the door was closed, Valentina's lips were on his, fierce and seeking.

It was like there was no thought or hesitation. No soft exploration. Gio grasped her thin waist and pinned her against the wall. He kissed her as if he were trying to swallow her whole. Valentina moaned into his mouth and began clawing at his shirt. She ripped it from him in one tug, nails dragging down his back.

"*Dio mio*," she panted, "you never change."

"Nor do you," Gio growled, spinning her toward the bed.

Unlike Franco's calculated style in the heat of a sports storm, there was no slowing down here. Gio wanted her, and she, him. Clothes littered the floor in a flurry of fabric. Gio's hands roamed not delicately but hungrily, grasping, tugging, and pinning. Every movement was firm and meant to demonstrate lustful power.

Valentina arched up into him, responding to his animalistic force with the same fervor. Their cadence was not gentle; it was raw, carnal—and hot. The room echoed with sharp gasps and ragged breaths, half pleasure, half submission.

She laced her strong legs around his waist, pulling him into her, into her tight heat. She bit at his shoulder as if to claim him. She was an inferno, a volcano, a fireball of pure unchecked emotion. Gio didn't ease off either; he only accelerated with more vigor, devouring her cries, hunting for his own release in a haze of need.

Eventually, they both landed on the bed, sweaty and spent. The candles had burned down in pools of wax. Valentina was tracing a finger down his chest, her smirk returning.

"You'll never quit me, writer boy," she whispered.

Gio knew she was right. For all Franco's wise words and all Gio's good sense, Valentina was his undoing. And he had allowed himself to be undone by her again.

Chapter 28

A Simmering Sauce Is Heating Up

Florence could muffle sound. Only the hum of late-night scooters on Via Roma and the odd click of a shutter as one of the cafés closed for the evening could be heard.

Gio walked alone on the lungarno. The cool night air hit his skin as he strode up and down. Half-distracted, half-watching, half-listening to the replay of the evening in his head.

Valentina's raw fire, her animal lust…He'd been wild that night, riding that rush, scraping along a razor's edge. There was risk with that fire, and part of him always felt relief, the fog of numbness. But relief was always chased by guilt.

He thought of Renata at La Terre Felice, her right to be there, Buca, and what was at stake. He knew his fun had a price, a ticking clock to the balance of pleasure and consequence. The give and take of playing outside the lines. One wrong word, one misstep and he could blow everything up; the balance of the estate and the people he cared about.

By dawn, he was on the road back. The Tuscan hills rose around him as the sun peaked over the vineyards. The car was familiar, and the winding roads calmed him, along with the smells, so familiar to him, of olive groves and cypress, and Antoinette's pots of early morning cooking hit his senses like a slap and a comfort.

Renata moved with quiet confidence throughout the property. She walked, checked the cottages, and looked in on the staff—suggesting minor adjustments, working collectively, while giving the agriturismo a running precision.

Antoinette watched her from a distance with pride. A woman comfortable in her inheritance and growing into it. Stepping beyond the day-to-day operations, Renata was learning the rhythm of La Terre Felice and owning it.

Gio gave her a moment to watch. It wasn't lost on him. The singular focus, the grace, the respect for the property. She was learning the estate, building the necessary credibility, trust, and connection to make this work. She wasn't just a name on paper.

Franco had slipped away the night before, back to the DP Tour. Before the rush of competition took him into the championship half of the season, before they became engulfed with their own events, there would be a moment. There would be a reckoning of attraction, tension, and desire. And he knew it was coming. He could see it on the horizon. A pause, a moment in the calm before the storm.

The stage was set. Renata's growth anchored the estate, Gio's resolve remained vigilant, and the threads of loyalty, ambition, and raw passion were poised to intertwine.

Chapter 29

The Confrontation

The scent of freshly roasted coffee beans and old wood greeted Luca as he stepped into the back room of the café in Florence. It was dark and Luca took a seat at the table in the corner, relaxed but on high alert.

He leaned back, arms crossed over his chest, enjoying the quiet of the place and feeling both comfort and familiarity that he hadn't experienced in quite some time. There was a time before La Terre Felice, long before the vineyard, long before most of the political happenings in Italy, that Luca spent many nights in places just like this.

Santino Buca was the one who walked in, scanning the room and making eye contact with Luca. They both had knowing looks, both on old times, old grudges, and both knew what the other could do to them. They were the old, and neither was stupid. They had both known each other before this, long before vineyards, long before anyone, and in a completely different field, but they were enemies, and neither forgot.

"Luca," Buca greeted, low, but with an edge of threat to it. "I did not expect to see you here."

"I know why I am here," Luca answered, voice low and steady. "And I do not have to tell you twice."

Buca smirked. "La Terre Felice…your employer's prize. Your friend's…legacy. You think you can protect it from me?"

Luca straightened, folding his arms over his chest. "I don't think. I know. And I will advise you not to test it."

There was a pause, a comfortable silence, between the two. It had not been the first time that they had stood across from one another, old and looking like they belonged in the place they were in. Both understood, both knew where the other stood. Buca chuckled, almost with a hint of malice, as he said, "We shall see how far loyalty can take you, Luca. We shall see how far anyone will fight to keep what is theirs."

Luca did not say anything. He just watched him, reading the man, taking in the tells, the stance, the barely veiled hostility. This was not over. No way. He knew this was just a beginning.

Buca rose from his seat, offering a slight salute before he left, and Luca let out a breath he didn't know he had been holding. He had the information he wanted, confirmation, and a reminder that it was very real. All around him. This was getting increasingly dangerous, and soon Luca would be ready.

Chapter 30

Safeguarding La Terre Felice

The sun rose and spilled across the olive groves, a clear sign that La Terre Felice was stirring to life, peacefully. Too quiet, too still, perhaps. There was a tension beneath the silence, and only Gio, Antoinette, and Luca could feel it.

They sat together at the long wooden table on the terrace, coffee steaming in front of them. Luca had returned from Florence late the night before, just before dawn. He was watchful, calm, but there was a sharpness to him, the shadows of the night still etched in his face.

It was Gio who spoke first, quietly, not as an accusation, but as a statement of fact. "You were in Florence."

Luca nodded once. "I had to see for myself. When you hear certain things, you don't always believe them. You must watch. Trust me, I know what's at stake."

Antoinette leaned forward, hands braced on the table in front of her. "Gio, Luca has always had our best interests at heart. He's meticulous. More than we like to admit, but always for the right reasons."

Gio studied them both, looking for the honesty in their eyes. "I know that. I always have. But I need to know that everything is safe here. La Terre Felice…everything we've built. Outsiders can't compromise it."

Luca's eyes darkened slightly. "It won't be. Not if we don't stay one step ahead. I know what I'm doing, and we can shore up every vulnerability."

Antoinette nodded, resolute. "We work together. Every day. Every little detail. Safety, security, vigilance. We leave no stone unturned."

Gio sighed, the weight of the moment settling over him. Relief, but also determination. "Alright. Then let's do it. Let's make this place safe, make it impossible to penetrate, for Gabby, for Renata, for everyone who calls La Terre Felice home."

The three of them shared a quiet understanding, an unspoken agreement that was stronger than words—the protection of La Terre Felice was a given.

As they rose from the table, the sun climbed higher in the sky, its light spilling over the vineyards, the cottages, the olive groves. La Terre Felice was at peace, but beneath the stillness, there was a readiness now—every stone, every path, every eye had been made alert.

Together, they set about planning for the day, quietly, deliberately, each one determined to protect the legacy they held so dear.

Chapter 31

Luca's Backstory Ties to Papal Intelligence

Luca grew up in Rome. And while his childhood had been sheltered in many ways, it was never completely normal. When other young Italians worked as tradesmen or scholars or dabbled in politics and the chasing of Italian women, Luca was selected for something different. Subtle.

After all, the Vatican had always protected its assets. During the uncertain and unstable decades following World War II, it had dusted off an ancient custom. The unobtrusive enlistment of custodi segreti, guardians of secrets.

The tradition was ancient. Popes utilized secret informants for centuries to watch over their domains and their interests. These networks were paid very well to guard the church's wealth and their position against nobles, foreign kings, and grasping cardinals of the church, along with every other powerful enemy.

Luca had been selected for this service, for this modern continuation of the network of men in black cassocks who had whispered in candlelit *palazzos* about the plans of princes and the plots of cardinals that threatened papal power.

He had been trained. He had learned about the Church's many precariously balanced defenses and the secret sins and hidden indulgences that had kept it standing through so much open persecution.

His tutors had spoken often of men like Cardinal Ippolito d'Este, who had done everything short of taking to the streets in a pope's costume to use his enormous palace in Tivoli and his patronage of Michelangelo to buy papal office for himself.

D'Este had been a failure as a candidate, a failure in the Vatican conclave six times over. He'd even lost one election by a single vote. But the point was not lost on him: the dangerous potential of unbridled influence, and those who would use it to their own ends without restraint.

Luca was a keen observer and a critical thinker even in his youth. He'd been selected for intelligence and had become a watcher, a man capable of entering a room in

Florence, Rome, or Naples and knowing what he needed to know.

He had never been an assassin, not even a soldier. But he was discreet, patient, and he had served with a quiet devotion to a church that had preserved his country for as long as he could remember.

The years of that service had cost him. Spying and conniving and silence had taken their toll, of course. He shed the life long ago, when he was no longer the right age for the custodi segreti network.

He eased back into civilian life a little worn and jaded by the knowledge of what men like him did in the shadows. It was a history only a handful of people, including Antoinette, knew; the reason the Rosettis had hired him years ago and why she never brought it up in jest.

And so, Santino Buca resurfaced. When the snippets of conversation Luca overheard at church and the market and the occasional fruitless investigations began to reveal just how much the man would sell himself for, how eager he was to build a family and lay hands on Gabby's money, to move with La Terre Felice into the kind of power that Luca once protected the Vatican against...

Antoinette knew just who to call. She had spent too long keeping secrets from Luca not to recognize just how the instincts she'd heard about from his friends in Vatican hallways and whispered in dark corners of rarefied church gatherings would be an asset in rooting out Buca.

Luca was no longer just a farmer. He was no longer just an older man to take comfort in during his waning years. He was a custodian of secrets, a man with an ancient faithfulness in his soul.

"I found it unnerving, Antoinette," Luca said. "The way Buca seems to have bought his way into a position of power in our region by a combination of gold and name. It's not unlike what I've been exposed to in the past."

"Except now," Antoinette said, "it's not the papacy you need to protect."

"It's the memory of Gabby. And the safety and security of La Terre Felice."

Chapter 32

Antoinette Serves Gio More Sauce

It was another hot, dry day at La Terre Felice. The evening was heavy. Gio and Antoinette sat on the stone terrace outside the farmhouse. Between them was a pitcher of sweet, iced tea. The only sounds were the clinking of their glasses.

Antoinette released a long, slow breath, like a deflating sigh. "Giovanni. Luca is more than what you see in front of you. He's lived …another life. A life that I've known about for years."

Gio swiveled in his seat, face-to-face with her. He looked past her; all he could see were images flashing through his head.

"What kind of life?" he asked.

She held his gaze with the piercing eyes of a true matriarch. "When he was younger, he worked in the service of the Vatican. Not as a priest. Not as a soldier. He was part of a secret brotherhood. Men who watched, reported, and if politics became too volatile, they'd ensure that the Church's interests were protected. Centuries ago, they were known as custodi segreti. Secret Keepers. Luca was one of them."

Gio pushed back in his chair. "A Vatican spy?"

Antoinette shook her head. "Not a spy, Giovanni. A protector. He watched men like Santino Buca long before either you or I had ever heard his name. Men who trade in riches and gold. In influence and power. Always hungry for more. He was trained to know the type."

Her eyes trailed back to Luca. He still stood in place, a sentinel against the night sky. "Buca knew him. Gio. That's why their meeting was abrupt. They know each other's history."

Gio took a slow drink of tea. Absorbing everything she was saying. "So, La Terre Felice isn't just another vineyard to Luca. He sees it like it's something he must protect."

Antoinette placed her hand over his. "Yes. When Mazocca tried to take this place from us, you and Franco protected it with the law. But men like Buca…if they can't own it, they will destroy it. Luca knows men like Buca. That's why I trust him."

Gio swallowed hard, struggling to focus on her words and the memory of Gabby and Renata and the inferno of heat that was all around him now…Buca, Valentina, Luca's past. "And you trust me to trust him?"

Antoinette smiled weakly, maternal but also with steel in her eyes. "I trust you to listen. To not see Luca as just an older man. But to see him as the watchman he has been all along. He has watched over secrets far greater than this. He has watched over Gabby's legacy. Over all of us."

The night air was deafeningly quiet. Gio felt both soothed and anxious at the same time. He realized, for the first time, La Terre Felice wasn't just a vineyard—it was a sanctuary, a treasure, and a target all at once.

Chapter 33

The Growing Tension Boils Over

The difference between professional golfers and everyone else is in their hands. Sure, their forearms are muscles chiseled out of solid iron, but those hands, scarred and roughened by the grip of tacky leather day after day, retain enough sensitivity to make a putter gently guide a golf ball to the bottom of the cup.

Franco had just returned from a couple of weeks on the DP Tour. Fifth place, and a tie for second. Half a million euros. His account was happy, but his body ached for rest from the time zones, the constant search for leads with Gio, and the lonely ghost of travel depression in his ears.

He needed a break.

She came in the middle of the night.

Renata opened the door to the private cottage at La Terre Felice with a single rap on the wood. Franco was surprised, but they had been exchanging coy, flirtatious, and sarcastically tinged notes for weeks.

"It's sexy how perceptive and brave you are, Renata," he whispered as she moved to close the space between them. Her skin was warm; her thin silk nightclothes clung to her, sticky as a sauna.

Franco had a feeling Renata had been more at home at the estate, helping with work and picking up the ins and outs of the agriturismo management from Luca, Antoinette, and the staff. She was finding her place, but for now, she needed to live.

She didn't say a word but rather just moved with a certainty of being the one in control of the situation, of knowing exactly what she wanted. Her slender body, the motion of her hips, and the shameless way she allowed his eyes to touch her said it all.

"Are you sure about this?" Franco asked as they were nearing the bed.

"I want you so badly, *campione*," she finally whispered. Then, the silk fell away, and she was at his belt as he shrugged off his shirt.

Franco was a master now. He slowed her down. Lips first, above her, then tracing kisses at the hollow of her neck, along her collarbone. On her arms. Those golfer's hands, at once so powerful and yet so precise, palmed her body like a familiar course charted long ago, lingering on every swell and dip. His fingers brushed her breasts, and his thumbs curled and tugged at her nipples, coaxing them firm.

The same hands that could beautifully cup a 7-iron could also trace the topography of her body. He knew where to linger, when to rub and tease, and when to move away. His touch slid down and down and down, enticing her wet warmth to open wide, teasing until she arched and a low, unshielded moan spilled from her lips.

Renata opened to him and surrendered the most personal of maps, and as they burned to the edge together, she crested over the point of no return. The sound she made was half-sob, half-victory, as if it were the release of years of tightness.

They did not stop. The night was theirs, and each took the time and the strength drawn from carnal honesty to give to the other, until the first light of dawn.

Spent, but very much alive in a way he had not felt in months, Franco pulled her close. "Ever since the moment I first saw you, Renata, I wanted to know you. You're one of those people who have this…presence. It's intelligent. And sexy as hell. And you know how to say the right thing at the right moment. Gio and I both see shades of Gabby in you."

"Speaking of Gio," Renata murmured, her finger tracing a long line across his chest, "how are we going to explain this to our scribe?"

"We'll let it stew," he said. "We've got enough fires to put out as it is."

Little did he know how significant those words would be.

"Franco, no man has ever touched me or made love to me with such passion and tenderness. I want more. I want to know you, and for you to know me. Are you ready for more?"

Before Franco could respond, the harsh clang of a bell and urgent shouts outside interrupted. The estate was awake, and something was very wrong down in the south vineyards.

Chapter 34
Farm to Table on Fire

The smell hit Gio first…smoke.

Luca's voice, cutting through the panic:

"Fire! South vineyard!" He roared, bounding toward the irrigation junction, fingers twisting the old brass levers to release the flow of water from hoses that snaked beneath the ground of the vineyard rows.

Luca and his crew were prepared. They had known the drought conditions were only going to worsen all summer. And while they had recently finished reinforcing and updating the irrigation lines for some of their most critical vineyard locations, they knew it was a stroke of luck for this day.

Gio ran to the ridge of land where he could make out the black pillar of smoke curling up to the sky. The vines were so dry and brittle from the drought; they were practically waiting for something to set them ablaze.

Antoinette barked orders at the kitchen staff as she slipped into action. Her apron was already splattered with dirt and soot. "Buckets! Pots! Anything that can hold water! Now!" she snapped as the team trudged dutifully forward to do her bidding.

Franco's voice boomed over the crackle of flames. "Line up! Don't let the fire jump the break!" He pushed the local villagers and tourists who had gathered to become the frontline. A human wall working to put distance between the fire and the rest of the vineyard.

Renata ran by, her hair wild, her face smeared with soot and ash, as she assisted Isabella in lugging hoses from the main cistern behind the house. The two women worked in tandem, but their arms shook from the weight of the water. Neither of them had ever had such a sudden lesson in emergency management, but there was no time to be fussy.

Gio hunkered down at the front line of the heat, chest tightening. The pop of burning shoots sounded like wails. "Gabby…no…not like this…" He muttered to himself as the taste of smoke stung.

Wind picked up, stirring embers and flying sparks. Luca's voice was again heard, short, with choppy Italian commands. He was now in full command, yelling orders back and forth, directing waterlines to pour onto one area of flames while others cycled through to keep the rows closest to the fire damp.

"Keep the rows wet!" He ordered. "If the roots survive, the vineyard survives!"

La Terre Felice had prepared. Months earlier, they cut firebreaks throughout their property. Barren strips of dirt cut through the rows to serve as containment to slow the rate of spread in the event of a fire. They had become a godsend. The fire crackled and roared in protest, but the breaks had forced it to jump rather than creep.

Still…it was almost upon them.

Gio's arms ached from hauling buckets, but he didn't stop. "Don't let it get to the top of the ridge!" He screamed.

Luca stopped for a moment in the smoke, eyes searching. On the far end of the vineyard, two men could be seen ducking into the shadows. One turned to face them. Luca sucked in a breath. He knew that face. But now was not the time. He would have time for revenge. Later.

For now, there was only survival.

Suddenly, like an act of god, the skies cracked open. Thunder boomed across the valley. A welcome symphony of fat, heavy raindrops soon followed…the first actual rain the area had seen in weeks. A collective sigh ran through the fields as water from the heavens joined their battle on the ground.

Fire hissed and sputtered in protest at the sudden assault. Within an hour, the towering inferno was reduced to small clumps of flame. The fire had jumped on a few acres in the bottom half of the vineyard, scorching and blackening many of the vines, but for the twenty-five acres that the south vineyard called home, this would be considered a win.

The roots had been protected. The water had kept the soil around them wet.

Renata fell to the dirt floor of the vineyard, chest heaving. Franco threw an arm around her shoulder as they both trembled from the effort and soot-stained smiles.

Antoinette dabbed ash from her cheeks with a sleeve. "*La mia famiglia*," she rasped. "We fight like family."

Gio stood, looking out across the blackened rows. Smoke curled into the newly wet air. La Terre Felice will be back. They had survived.

But as Luca watched the trail left by the two men disappearing into the woods, he knew the fire had not been an accident.

If they could not have La Terre Felice, they would come to destroy it.

And Luca would not rest until he made sure of their consequence.

Chapter 35

Ashes and Resolve

The day after the fire dawned still and silent. Smoke drifted slowly on the southern slope as if it had yet to accept its banishment. A fine ash lay on the vines and the stone walkways, in the air itself.

Gio stalked between the rows, heavy-booted and walking with the slow, melancholy slouch of a man who had seen his home reduced by fire. Kneeling, he pressed his hand to the soil; it was hot, but not dead.

"La Terra Felice lives," he said softly. "So will we."

Behind him, a shirtless Franco approached, his arms blackened and torn. "The last embers are out," he said. "The fire crews were amazed. It's a miracle. The wind shifted just in time."

"A miracle, or something else," Gio murmured, casting a look toward the slope where Luca had shouted instructions the night before.

Antoinette was already at work, barking orders at the kitchen staff with military precision.

Platters of bread and cheese, bowls of hot stew were being wheeled out to where the volunteers huddled. "Eat first," she barked at anyone who approached for orders. "We rebuild on a full stomach."

Renata, scarf tied back on her head, walked through the vineyard with a clipboard in hand. Her staff marked out sections of damage assessment. She stopped frequently, running gentle fingers over the vines, murmuring small prayers. She continued without pausing when Gio joined her at her side, her eyes weary and yet, Gio thought, resolute.

"The roots are good," she said. "Look here? Burnt above the ground, but the soil is still fertile. They will come back if we give them time."

Gio nodded, a surge of pride and relief swelling in his chest. "You sound like Gabby," he said, almost to himself.

Renata smiled faintly. "She was right. Roots that survive fire grow deeper and stronger."

Later that day, the group gathered at the long oak table in the tasting room. The air was heavy with the smell of smoke and coffee. Luca, freshly bathed and changed, presented a tight-lipped map of the day's work.

"The irrigation system did its job," he began. "We lost a few acres, give or take. The south vineyard only. The firebreaks held."

Franco joined him. "The locals brought help faster than the brigade. All the village. Some of the tourists, too."

Antoinette folded her hands. "Because this place fills more than bellies," she said. "They know that."

Gio leaned forward. "What about cause?"

Luca paused. "Dry season. Wind. May have been a spark from machinery."

Gio considered him. "May have been."

Their eyes met and held, one long, silent beat passing between them. Luca's face did not flinch, but his tone softened when he spoke. "Some questions can be answered at a later time."

Renata looked from one to the other, the space of unspoken words hovering between them. "Whatever it was," she said, "we do not stop. We rebuild."

Luca gave a faint nod. "*Si, Signorina*. But we look forward, with open eyes."

That night, the four of them stood on the terrace and watched a light rain begin to fall. It was as if the sky itself had joined them in a final, cleansing act of absolution.

Franco put a hand on Renata's shoulder, small and almost unconscious, but Gio saw it, saw the way she leaned back into him. It was not the connection of mere gratitude and happenstance, but something new and alive and growing in both. The unmistakable warmth of two souls having crossed a line that neither intended to cross.

Antoinette saw it too but said nothing. Instead, she turned away, granting Gio the silence he needed.

Later, when the others went inside, Gio remained on the terrace with Franco.

"She means something to you," Gio said softly.

Franco met his gaze. "More than I expected. I did not plan it, Gio. It just…happened."

Gio exhaled, looking out at the smoldering vineyard. "Life has a way of happening like that. She carries a part of Gabby with her. You guard that with your life."

"I will," Franco said. "You have my word."

Gio placed a hand on his shoulder. "Then you have my blessing."

Franco nodded once, and they understood. Brothers, friends, survivors.

Thunder rumbled in the distance, a long, rolling cry on the Tuscan hills. Inside, laughter was again being raised from the kitchen. The storm would pass, the vines would heal, and life, strong as ironwood, would continue at La Terre Felice.

Chapter 36

Shadows Among the Vines

The rain had come early, cleansing the worst of the smoke from the air. It was wet and smelled of earth and burnt straw, but it was alive. The south vineyard was blackened but still breathing; like a soldier who'd survived battle and now stood wounded, but unbroken.

The rest of the estate slept, exhaustion finally winning out. All except Luca.

He moved through the rows, light off, just the pale silver of the moon to guide him. His steps were silent, deliberate, the walk of someone who knew the way. He heard every sound in that old part of his brain that never truly slept.

He came to the far side of the vineyard where the stone wall met the old olive grove. That was where he'd seen them…two dark shapes against the flame, one carrying what looked like a fuel canister. It wasn't random. The fire had started there.

Luca dropped to one knee, examined the ground. He touched the soil, the scorched edge of a vine post, the flattened grass where boots had pressed down. He found it, what he was looking for: cigarette butts, three of them, the cheap disposable kind that men who couldn't afford good tobacco preferred.

He tucked one in his pocket and slipped back toward the estate, walking the perimeter until he came to the terrace. The moonlight struck his face, but there was no fear in him, only calculation.

He'd seen one of them before—Santino Buca's driver. The thought returned to him like an aftertaste: the narrow eyes, the crooked ear, the lopsided walk of someone used to following orders.

Later that morning, Luca met Gio and Antoinette in the office. Antoinette was poring over the insurance paperwork, while Gio leaned by the window with a large shot of espresso, staring at the hills stained with smoke.

Luca said softly, "The fire was not of nature."

Gio turned, eyes narrowing. "Are you sure?"

"I am."

Antoinette hardened. "Who?"

Luca paused, took a moment. "Old friends of a man we met in Florence. They were sloppy. They wanted damage. Not death."

Gio frowned, "Why start something they can't finish? Legally, La Terre Felice is locked down. Papered over."

Luca met his gaze, those steady brown eyes. "When men can't have something, they often prefer to see it burn."

Antoinette's voice was quiet, "Buca?"

Luca didn't confirm, but the silence between them was answer enough. That evening, he took a walk into the small nearby village of Montepulciano, down its narrow cobbled streets, where every door had its own story. He stopped outside a low tavern, an old place that only served those who knew what to ask for.

Inside, a few locals played cards, their faces familiar, but two men sitting in the corner stiffened as Luca came in. Luca gave a small nod to the barkeep, a signal that passed in the room like smoke.

He took a table by the window and ordered a glass of Vin Santo and waited. One of them—the man with the crooked ear—eventually approached.

"You looking for someone, old man?" The thug said, in a thick Italian dialect.

Luca smiled faintly. "No. But I did see your handiwork last night. You've gotten careless."

The man straightened. "You should forget what you think you saw."

"Perhaps," Luca said. "But if I forget, others won't. You've played with fire on land that doesn't belong to you. The next time you come near it, you won't walk away."

The man sneered, "You think you scare me?"

Luca leaned close. "I don't need to scare you. I only need to remind you I was watching long before you were born."

Something in his voice made the man hesitate. He said something under his breath to his partner, and the two slipped away into the night.

Luca finished his drink slowly, left a few euros on the table, and stepped back out into the street.

Back at La Terre Felice, the air felt lighter, but the peace was fragile. He knew that this was not the end. Buca would come again, something more insidious next time. Still, as Luca watched the morning light stretching across the hills, he allowed himself one small comfort. He'd kept his promise to Antoinette. The family was safe. For now.

He looked toward the vines and allowed himself to hope that new shoots would soon push through the blackened stems.

"Faith and roots," he said, low. "That's all that ever saves us."

Chapter 37

La Stazione Ferroviaria

Luca walked in the vineyard at dawn, through a light fog still rising from the ashes. The land would heal. The vines would heal. They always did, sooner or later, like people. But some things had to be taken care of from the root up.

The people he'd seen the night of the fire weren't ghosts. They were as much flesh and blood as he was, and they'd made a big mistake.

By noon, Luca had made his calls. No, not to the police. Not to anyone who would make a report. The old segreti network. Men who owed him favors from a lifetime ago, who kept their mouths shut, who moved with efficiency. Quietly. No noise. No trace. Just business.

Buca and his driver had been out by Siena on the edge of town, trying to slip away back to Florence. Luca was waiting. Smiling pleasantly to himself, the storm behind his eyes was hidden by his mask of calm.

"Signor Buca," Luca said softly, "you have been expected. There is a train leaving soon."

Buca's smirk went sour when he took in the two men behind Luca, silent and unblinking, unmoving as marble statues.

The driver shuffled nervously.

Buca sighed and drew in a deep breath. "You don't understand…"

"Oh, I do," Luca said calmly. "You set fire to sacred ground; you put family and the entire village in danger. That, I cannot forgive."

Luca gestured at the car idling behind him. "Come. Let's get you on that train."

Hours later, as dusk fell over La Terre Felice, Luca returned on foot. The faint stench of smoke was finally gone, replaced by the sweet aroma of crushed grapes. The south vineyard looked as though the land itself had been scorched, black in some places, and marred in others. But the vines were still standing. They were alive.

Antoinette was waiting at the gate, an expression of understanding on her face.

"It's done?" she asked.

Luca nodded once. "They're gone. To the stazione."

She crossed herself silently and then turned away toward the lights of the kitchen. "Then let's begin again."

By the morning, the hum of La Terre Felice began to pick back up. The south vineyard was blackened in spots, but it had not yet been broken. Workers moved through the rows systematically, clearing out the charred remains of years and testing the irrigation system. Small green shoots still poked through the ash, new life in a field of death; small miracles that reminded everyone of why they were fighting so hard.

Gio wandered through the rows in silence, running his fingers over the ruined earth, tracing the pockets of damage, feeling the strange weight of loss and the reassurance of relief that came after.

Something had shifted, he knew, not just in the soil but in the very air.

Franco came up behind him with a clipboard of notes, and Renata was in close pursuit. They spoke softly—among the sound of shovels scraping in the dirt—of replanting schedules and water tables and soil regeneration, but Gio's eyes kept catching the way her hand lingered on Franco's arm. He said nothing at first, just smiled faintly.

"So…La Terre Felice can be a sort of union in more ways than one."

Franco hesitated; the confident golfer suddenly became more than a little awkward. Renata blushed.

He placed a hand on Franco's shoulder. "She's a good one. Don't lose sight of that, or what we've built here."

Franco nodded and mouthed a silent thank you. Renata's eyes glistened, not with shame, but with relief. For the first time since the fire, the vineyard was awake.

Later, Gio caught Luca near the olive grove, watching from the shadows with his hands clasped behind his back. He was staring off toward the hills, as if in meditation. Something had settled about him; not quite peace exactly, but resolution.

Gio approached slowly, wary of startling him. "You didn't sleep much, either, I imagine."

Luca gave him a quick look. "Some things can only be taken care of at night."

They both looked to the east, where the sun was just beginning to rise.

"The danger's passed," Luca added, glancing at Gio. "You can put your energy back into rebuilding. It's safe now. The land's safe."

Gio studied him for a long moment and then nodded. "Good. That's all I needed to know."

As the morning breeze rolled in, raking the last of the ash out to the perimeters, Gio felt it return to him, something that had been missing. Maybe once more, the feeling of belonging, of unfinished purpose. La Terre Felice had been through the fire, and it had come out the other side.

The vines would heal. Everyone would heal.

As the workers filed in for lunch and the last of the ash was raked away, Gio lingered by the south vineyard, staring. The soil was still warm underfoot as though the land itself still held the memory of the fire. He bent and scooped up a handful of dirt, watching as the black dust ran through his fingers and fell away to reveal the brown below. Life beneath loss.

He could almost hear Gabby's voice riding on the breeze, a whisper to the earth: *"The land remembers who loves it."*

Gio raised his head, gazing out over the fields, past the olive grove where Luca's shadow disappeared into the sunlight, and another walk with Isabella. Franco and Renata were at the far end near the terrace, moving together through the sunbreak, laughter bubbling as he watched, replacing the silence that had lingered for so long. Antoinette moved quietly and with command among the vines, at work as usual and as steady as ever, a force of nature as much as Luca was.

La Terre Felice had not only survived fire. It had survived greed, grief, and ghosts.

And somehow, it had been born anew.

He whispered to the wind, to Gabby, to the very land itself,

"We're still here. And we're not done yet."

Chapter 38

Renata's Rise

Weeks later, the south vineyard was still a blackened skeleton of charred posts and mangled wire, spindly trellises, and singed leaves. Young green shoots, though, were already pushing through the ground.

Renata strolled through the rows with Antoinette and Luca in the mornings, clipboard in hand, a straw hat pulled low over her icy blues. She moved with a new confidence. She no longer carried the uncertainty that had made her so pensive in the past. She was a businesswoman, after all, with her shop in Siena before everything changed in her life.

As morning moved into early afternoon, the courtyard filled with the scent of rosemary, garlic, and tomatoes on the stove. Antoinette had been insistent on a "proper" meal…*"to remind the land and the people that we are alive."*

They sat around the long farmhouse table, Antoinette at one end and Gio on the other, with Renata tucked between Franco (who had returned from a few tournaments) and Isabella. Luca was the last to arrive, sleeves rolled up, bottles of deep ruby-red Brunello in his hands.

The first cork popped with a wet hiss.

"These are from the 2016 harvest," Luca said. "A survivor, like us," as he poured.

Antoinette raised her glass. "To La Terre Felice, and to what endures."

The dinner progressed at a typical Tuscan leisurely pace: roasted chicken with fresh garden herbs, a platter of grilled peppers drizzled with oil, bread still warm from the oven. Glasses were refilled, and there was laughter between mouthfuls of food. For the first time in a long while, the afternoon had a lightness, not the tension that had permeated their days since the fire.

Franco leaned toward Renata. "You didn't just rebuild vines," he said. "You gave us all something to breathe for."

Renata smiled. "I just listened to the rhythm of this place. It tells you what you need to do."

Isabella laughed across the table at something Luca whispered. She met Renata's eye, a flash of recognition between two women who had lost so much and yet were still here in the brightest of light.

Gio watched it all: the flirting, the toasts, the playful brushes of memory and celebration. He pulled back in his chair, his eyes taking it all in. Gabby's chair sat empty at the table, but you could feel her everywhere in the room.

Outside, after dinner, lanterns were lit. The courtyard glowed in the twilight.

Gio took a solitary walk down the path to the olive grove. The air smelled of new life, of the earth. He stopped beneath the tree where he had proposed to Gabby. The land, alive again. Reborn.

He could hear voices from the house, drifting down the path to him—Renata's, clear and determined; Antoinette's, bright and steady; Franco's, low and easy-going. Luca's rich baritone joined them, and Isabella's more breathy inflection wrapped around it.

Gio smiled.

This place was not just surviving. It was evolving.

He looked up to the stars. *"You were right, amore,"* he whispered. *"The land always knows who and what it needs."*

Back inside, Gio's notebook sat open on the kitchen counter next to a cold Limoncello. A few pages had scrawled notes about an island, a volcano, and the resilient people who lived in the shadow of both.

He closed the cover softly. The road would be calling soon enough.

But for now, he listened to the laughter from the courtyard, drank his after-dinner liquor, and settled into the peace of La Terre Felice.

Chapter 39

The Roots of Companionship

Yet another day had dawned, and with it another golden sky. Harvest was approaching, and the vineyards were bursting with their burden of fruit.

Inside the farmhouse, the strains of a song from the old gramophone were spilling out from open windows onto the terrace—*Nessun Dorma* by Puccini.

Isabella was at the kitchen counter, setting a plate with figs and pecorino, humming to herself. Luca entered the room silently from the opposite direction, drawn in by the sound of music. He'd grown accustomed to the way the air around Isabella always seemed to carry a hint of rosemary and olive oil.

"Puccini again?"

"Always." Isabella smiled, topping the plate off with figs. "His music is a reminder to me that passion doesn't get extinguished by age, it just gets more patient."

Luca laughed. "The words of a woman who has lived and loved and done so wisely."

They sat down on the terrace overlooking the valley, with a bottle of chilled Vernaccia between them. For a time, neither spoke. They didn't need to. There had long since been no shortage of words between the two of them. Instead, there had become a comfortable silence in its place. An unspoken rhythm of two people who had been through enough of life's storms to know when the breeze had stopped blowing.

"I used to listen to Verdi," Luca murmured. "In the long nights. When the work I was doing…the people I was watching…when it all seemed to weigh on me. Music was a reminder that there was still beauty left in the world."

Isabella nodded, eyes on the horizon. "After Gio's father left, and I found myself with a little boy and no sense of purpose, it was the opera I would put on late at night. Tosca, *La Traviata*… the voices were reminders that love and loss are forever dance partners."

He reached over, fingers brushing across her hand. "Then we have a lot more in common than most."

The gramophone crackled softly, and the familiar melody of *O Mio Babbino Caro* swelled in the air around them. Isabella smiled, distant. "Ah, my favorite. When I hear this, I feel as young as I used to be. Like I could run through the vineyards barefoot, my hair all in the wind."

Luca poured the last of the wine. "Perhaps you still could be."

She laughed, the sound like it belonged in this place.

Stars came out one by one in the sky, on the hilltop above. Lights flickered in the distance from the newly restored south vineyard. A reminder of what they had all fought so hard to save.

The final notes played on, slow and lingering, and Isabella turned to Luca. "You have brought peace to this house again. Antoinette is the matriarch, Gio has his stories, Franco has his golf, and Renata has a reconnection to her heritage. But you…you have brought protection."

Luca smiled, touched. "And you, Isabella, have given me something that I thought I lost long ago. A true sense of belonging."

The two sat side by side, hands linked, listening as Puccini's song floated out into the olive groves; two hearts in accord, both grateful for the music that had always been their solace.

Gio watched from the window inside, unseen. He smiled slightly, not in amusement, but rather in understanding. In a house where love and loss had once taken root, a different kind of warmth and connection had quietly grown.

Chapter 40

Gio's Table Is Reset

The next morning, Gio stood on the terrace with a cup of espresso, watching the first workers move through the rows of vines. The south vineyard, once nearly lost, shimmered with new growth.

He'd memorized every stone, every vineyard and grove, every leaf of La Terre Felice. For the first time in his life, he thought, I could let you breathe without me.

Renata's laughter sounded from the courtyard as she greeted the field hands. Her energy gave tempo to the day. Inside the house, Luca, Isabella, and Antoinette cleared breakfast dishes. The comfortable music of their voices echoed from the kitchen.

Gio sipped his espresso, letting the flavor burn all the way down. The grief that had hung on him since Gabby's death—the shame of not being there when he should have been—dissipated slowly with each new sound of returning life on the property. Gabby's dream had not died. It had simply evolved. And Renata was the secret sauce ingredient that changed everything.

He packed his small leather bag that afternoon, the same one he'd carried across Europe for years. Laptop and notebook were inside, the former with a blank screen, the latter with blank pages. Before leaving, Gio walked from the courtyard and olive grove up the hill. The air smelled of rain-soaked earth.

"È ancora la tua terra," he murmured. *"It's still your land, Gabriella."*

He was on a plane that afternoon, and then on the ferry to Sicily, watching the island's silhouette appear in the distance—rugged, ancient, and as varied as its people.

Taormina was his first destination, a place Gabby had always loved. Below the cliffs, the Ionian Sea was like a vat of molten glass. He rented a small room above a café, opened his laptop, and began to write.

He wrote of the mountain—Etna, breathing and alive, destroyer and giver. Of the hundred villages clinging to its foothills, where farmers, winemakers, and shepherds lived in harmony with the relentless rhythm of creation and eruption. For centuries, life was born from fire.

It was a story few knew: the power of the people who didn't live in fear of Etna, but in union with 'The Idol.'

Late that night, Gio sent a text to La Terre Felice:

"The table is set once again. I'll see you in a few weeks in Taormina—for Gabby."

He closed his laptop, gazed at the faint red glow in the distance, and smiled.

This time, he wasn't running from his past. He was writing toward the future.

Chapter 41

Let's Celebrate and Feast on Life

A special night in a special place was on deck as the notes of a distant mandolin drifted across the piazza. For the first time in months, Gio felt a quiet stillness in his chest.

Footsteps on cobblestones brought his attention up and out. Antoinette, Franco, Renata, Luca, Isabella, and the rest of their crew walked toward the square, their voices and laughter spilling out into the night air.

Years weighed heavily on each of them, yet their eyes glowed with the resiliency and love that had pulled them all to La Terre Felice, and Gabby.

He stood, motioning to each person with a warm embrace.

"*Bellissimo*," Isabella murmured, her eyes crinkling with delight. "It's like we brought La Terre Felice with us."

Renata grinned, her arm interlocking with Franco's. "And tonight, we celebrate Gabby in all the ways she would have wanted."

The second anniversary of Gabby's celebration of life was on the agenda in Taormina. The crown jewel on the east coast of Sicily was her favorite place to visit outside of La Terre Felice. Traditional Sicilian culture with a side of artistic Greek influence and a ripe, healthy tourist trade had always been a magical place for her. Even more so with the combined energy of the sea and the mountain.

"Good food, good wine, a birds-eye view of fiery Etna, and our La Terre Felice family. What more could we ask for to celebrate Gabby?" Gio announced. "Nothing, nothing at all," all agreed.

They were all meeting at a favorite on the Via Leonardo da Vinci. Ristorante Incanto provided its famous dishes with a Mediterranean seafood twist. The restaurant's cozy vibe was fitting for the small group, and the only thing anyone wanted to do was talk, celebrate life, and move on to the next chapter in their lives.

Luca was present with Isabella, of course, with Gio's blessing. This new relationship was a thing of beauty, as nearly two septuagenarians found each other and loving companionship later in life.

Renata and Franco were the new item, most unexpectedly and serendipitously. Franco was on top of the world: a big year of winnings on the pro tour, and a brewing romance.

"I had a big year, Amici miei," he boomed. "This night is on me!"

"It's about time you paid for something, Franco Reno," Gio shot back.

The patrons at the table laughed uproariously and clinked glasses in a toast to life and the future.

"*Alla nostra,*" they all said in unison.

Paolo, Maria, and Sofia were also invited and had made the trip to the island. While Sofia manned the bar, marketing La Terre Felice to anyone who would listen, Antoinette sat at the head of the table. She was the matriarch and always on duty when it came to her staff and family.

They ate, drank wine, and lost themselves in their togetherness.

This is what Gabby would have wanted, Gio thought. Not just memories, but life—fully lived and fiercely cherished.

Gio broke his thought with an announcement.

"I have a surprise," he said. "I was able to secure tickets to tonight's concert at Teatro Antico. IL Volo is in the house. It will be magnificent and a night to remember."

"*Bellissimo, Gio,*" Antoinette chimed. "*Bravo, paisan,*" Franco added.

They ambled over to the ancient Greek Theatre on Via Teatro Greco, which dates to the third century AD. It's one of the oldest outdoor venues in Magna Graecia, featuring a curved seating area. Behind the curtain on the stage is a stunning visual. The city lights' beauty with the peaks of Mt. Etna as a backdrop. The Greeks knew how to create art.

On this night, Etna, once again spewed fire, illuminated the night sky in a glowing orange-red hue as IL Volo opened the concert with "Now We are Free," the theme from *Gladiator*. The crowd roared.

Chills went through Gio as Etna rumbled with the music, and he thought back to that night two years ago when Etna exploded. Was it eerily coincidental, or was Gabby's spirit alive and present? He honored that thought yet also knew he had to move forward with his passion for writing and storytelling.

IL Volo, the three young Italian tenors, mesmerized the crowd with their blend of classical theatre, opera, and pop renditions, all culminating in a crowd favorite. "O Solo Mio" begins to echo throughout the hills as Etna breathes its fire and ash.

Gabby is watching and blessing this night, Gio whispered to himself.

"Che bella cosa na jurnata 'e sole,
n'aria serena doppo na tempesta!
Pe' ll'aria fresca pare gia' na festa
Che bella cosa na jurnata 'e sole.

Ma n'atu sole
cchiu' bello, oi ne'.
'O sole mio
sta 'nfronte a te!
'O sole, 'o sole mio
sta 'nfronte a te
sta 'nfronte a te!"

Chapter 42

Leaving the Tiramisu, Chasing the Adventure

As the song played to its close, Gio stood, collecting his things.

The buzz about Gio's work on Mt. Etna and the villages and people that drew strength from living on its foothills was from both history enthusiasts and high travel organizations. Gio had been given a huge offer to travel the world to write about people, places, and adventures that needed their stories told.

"I am going with what I know how to do," he said. "I'm a vagabond and need to travel and see the world again. La Terre Felice is safe. Antoinette is running it. Renata's piece is solid. When Antoinette signs, it's done. All of you will share in Gabby's legacy."

Gio turned to Isabella. "Mamma, promise me a seat at the table when I get back to La Terre Felice. "Isabella coughed and choked on tears, "I am so proud of you, Giovanni. Go. Make us prouder. I will be here when you return."

Franco launched into a bear hug around Gio. "Stay sharp out there, paisan," reminded Franco. "I will, *mio fratello, da un'altra madre*. Please don't make the mistake I did. Take good care of this beauty and keep her safe and secure."

Renata pulled Gio into a long embrace, her icy blues liquefying in the moment's emotion. "I love you so much, my storyteller," she said in a whisper. "Thank you for listening to Gabby and following your curious heart. I know she would have wanted this. You have made her proud."

There wasn't a dry eye in the group, including Gio's. As he stood to leave, he made sure they all knew how he felt.

"*Ciao, arrivederci, mi famiglia*," he said. "My love for you all is boundless."

Gio then slipped out of the theatre gathering while the crowd stood in unison to proclaim their affection for the tenors.

The air was cool outside, salted by the sea. From below, the voices from Teatro Antico came up the hillside, a last whisper of song hanging in the air.

She stood in the half-light, petite, regal, and so sure, leaning against the stone wall. Gio saw the shape before the face. Trouble and history and gravity, all in one profile.

"Only you leave during the encore," she said, not quite smiling.

"Only you wait in doorways," he replied.

A beat too long, all the history between them jostling for the space, Gio shouldered his bag.

"I'm leaving," he said.

"I know," she acknowledged, stepping closer to him. "Then grant me an hour."

He knew better. He went anyway.

They slipped into the alley, swallowed by the dark, while Etna pulsed red on the distant horizon.

Epilogue

I debated this ending for a while and wrote the last two chapters before leaving for Southern Italy. During the trip, I got the clearest sign this was the ending I was supposed to use.

On the last full day touring Southern Italy, I booked a massage at our hotel's thermal spa on the island of Ischia. The young therapist fit me into her schedule, and after two weeks of cobblestone walking, it was exactly what I needed.

"*Come ti chiami?*" I asked, trying to be friendly.

"Valentina," she answered.

"*E tu?*" she asked.

"Giovanni," I said.

Now, that may not seem like anything, but in the context of both novellas, it was a clear sign to me that the ending of *It's Sauce, Not Gravy!* had to stay, telling me to keep the story open to more adventures for our wanderlust travel writer.

Once again, Gio meets an attractive Valentina. Only this time it was real.

What are the odds of these same names meeting in this encounter on Ischia Island in Italy?

Off the betting charts! I'm convinced there was a reason besides simple serendipity.

Truth is saucier and stranger than fiction…

Acknowledgments

I f you're still reading this, thank you. For taking the time, for caring, and for going on this journey with Gio and the rest of the La Terre Felice family.

Writing these stories was more than I'd bargained for. It became a chance to remember who I am and where I come from.

Each chapter reminded me of the sights, sounds, and tastes of Italy I grew up in: the heat, the attitude, and the noisy passion of Southern Italy, where my family comes from. Every page brought me closer to that rhythm: the laughter at the table, the scent and taste of Sunday meals, and the meaning of home—even when life and ambition pull you elsewhere.

The good news is that the celebration of food, the rituals, and the heritage remain the foundation of my life, and they still find their way into my fiction, one way or another.

I never intended to write two novellas that would bring me this close to home again – but they did exactly that. And in Gio, Gabby, Antoinette, Isabella, Franco, Luca, Renata, and the rest of the La Terre Felice crew, I found a part of myself I didn't even know was lost.

To my family—past, present, and those whose names may have faded with time—thank you for giving me roots deep enough to regrow and dreams wide enough to chase.

To Italy…for your soul, your madness, and your beauty, and for being the place that gives me the greatest inspiration and connection to life I could ever hope for.

And to you, the reader…*Grazie!*

Your time and imagination are gifts I'll never take for granted. I hope these journeys offered a nostalgic happiness, an escape, a spark of warmth in your heart, or, at the very least, made you hungry for your own adventure.

After all, that's what La Terre Felice—the Tuscan agriturismo—is about: finding joy wherever life places you…and never forgetting where you came from.

Until next time, *ciao e grazie di cuore. (thank you from the bottom of my heart).*

About the Author

J.A. Marz is a healthcare marketing and branding strategist, content consultant, and author whose work sits at the crossroads of story and strategy. His debut novel, *Ciao, Amore Mio…The Tale of Gabby and Gio—An Italian Discovery* was released in 2025 and explores love, loss, and self-discovery with warmth, honesty, and an unmistakable Italian spirit.

His sequel, *It's Sauce, Not Gravy!* continues the story, diving deep into identity, belonging, and the ties that hold people and families together.

J.A. holds a Bachelor of Arts degree from Commonwealth University–Bloomsburg in Pennsylvania and earned an Executive Leadership Certificate from Georgetown University's Center for Professional Development in Washington, DC. He lives in the Lehigh Valley, PA, never far from a good espresso, a family recipe, or a well-told tale.

www.ingramcontent.com/pod-product-compliance
Lightning Source LLC
Chambersburg PA
CBHW060326310726